HEAVEN:

ONE GIRL'S IMAGINATION

GWENDOLYN L WILKINSON

TABLE OF CONTENT

INTRODUCTION

1 Corinthians 13:12 "Now we see but a poor reflection as in a mirror; then we shall see face to face. Now I know in part; then I shall know fully, even as I am fully known." [NIV]

Introduction

HUMC
Emmaus Walk
November 2009

I don't know the time because they took away my watch, removed all the clocks, and even sneaky former pilgrims now employed at the church did things to mess with my mind! Like working in other offices when we were to pass by – sneaky – does that sound like good Christian people to you. Actually, I'm mad because it took me until she told me to figure it out! I wish I had thought of it!

I was mad at God the whole weekend because they put me at the wrong table. Actually, I don't think it was the wrong table group – we were just named wrong. We were supposed to be Esther – she is adopted, a Queen, "for such a time as this" – that is me.

Hello, God were you paying attention up there! Maybe you missed all the prayers from family, friends, HUMC Prayer Team and my personal prayer guru.

All weekend we took turns figuring things out and countered each other with "participate, NOT anticipate". It became one of many inside jokes. Our table was closest to the "Servants" – yeah right – they are the clergy and leaders – we are the troublemakers. God, you couldn't even find new clergy to be the spiritual director. It's one of my former associate pastors. Come on. I've only been an United Methodist for 7 years. Only had 4 associates and you had to pick one of the four. Then you place the Laity Director's Pilgrim in the chair to my left. On my right is a woman, who reminds me of a version of myself except we have nothing in common : occupation, martial status, education, children.

We experienced weirdness beyond belief from the first moments. If my daddy allowed me to believe in coincidences – I would say they just happened. But he has told me since I was 5 about my adoption story, God is behind these moments. "Ah ha" Moments I later heard them called. We were even having the same "ah ha" moments then turning to each other and saying "Did that just happen?". I have never had group "ah ha" moments. I wonder if that's normal at Emmaus. I'm going to add it to the many list of questions that I keep.

But now it's over.

They come back from a chapel to eat ice cream. One of the first to leave chapel – not sure what to do or when to leave so I leave when I see a few people leave – I'm probably one of the first 10 people back. The table starts to return their talking about thoughts. They asked me what the experience reminded me of – I say "Home". They look shocked and disappointed. I'm looking around and listening to them – they start talking about how that must be how heaven is. I'm thinking "really". I don't see heaven that way at all. But I don't say anything. Maybe heaven is different for everyone - or maybe shock beyond shock – I might be wrong – I am usually right, almost always.

Now, I'm doubting God's ability to even put the team together and work these "ah ha" moments in. I need some strong drugs or laughter…one. Since I like control so much, that leaves me with laughter, okay…seems God's saw my confusion. A teammate asks "what's next"; only to told "Bed". She just finished a big bowl of ice cream and caffeine-laced drink. It's hysterical! I wish I could tell her story but that's hers to tell. You would scream over her "white fuzzy slippers".

My teammate and I are also roommates – we are walking back to the room. She says "I wonder which pajamas I should wear tonight?". Okay, I've been coveting her cute pjs all weekend. "My name is Gwen and I still struggle with the big 10. Coveting is my new favorite until God speaks to me about it – I get to keep it – it takes 3 sermons to confirm it – then I'll have to give it up. It's a rule. Just ask Pastor D, she made the rule for the spiritual hypochondriac that thought every sermon was directed at her (i.e. me). Of course, I'm an overachiever so I try to listen after 2 times.

Okay back to this question of heaven. What do I imagine it to be ?

I really don't know when or how I will go . But without a doubt, I have a picture of what it will be like. People say that your relationship with your earthly dad, daddy, or Father colors how you picture God. I think it to be true but not just your earthly dad, daddy, or Father but your mom, brothers, sisters, aunts, uncles, grandparents, cousins, friends, and associates. As an adopted child, or "chosen child", being adopted by God and "joint heirs with Jesus" is a very easy concept for me to understand.

It's just the law.

So if you read The Shack, you will know that the author drew a picture of God that made sense to the man in the story. If you haven't read The Shack, stop reading this and pick up that book. It's deep and hard but it's worth it. Plus you will need lighter reading after that one!

In my story, my references to the THREE persons in familiar, nicknames, fashion is not intended to diminish the Holy, Majestic, Awe-inspiring nature of God. To be honest, it's hard for me to grasp it all at the same time because I'm human. I haven't figured out all the pieces yet NOR do I think I'm supposed to down here. It's something that I've added to my "Little Black Bag" that will be waiting on me in heaven so I can search for the answers there. If I come to an event or scripture that doesn't make sense at the time, I just have Holy Spirit add it to my little black bag.

For example, I wonder why in the world a specific manager told me over and over again "Gwen, you don't have to be perfect you just have to be the best." When I have shared it w/ co-workers, they were amazed. In fact, he told them the numbers had to be perfect. Now it's not something I'm going to email or call him about here on earth because he might not remember it and he might not know why he told me that. I have it in my black bag because I want God to explain why it was me that he told - because I think God will understand why I needed to hear that. The manager probably doesn't even remember it – which is the reason I will not give his name.

I need a sip of Iced Tea!

This fairy tale is based on my own experience so I have used real people and things around me. Your experience and ideas will be different from mine because of the things that shaped you.

Are you ready? I really did take a drink of iced tea before I started typing again!

Drum Roll, please. I think the opening credits are finally over…and the main attraction is about to begin…now presenting THE SLIDE…

The Slide

Aside :
"Peter, the head office just called. We have a slider. We are to open the gates and move out of the way. "
"Great. I have this job but I never get to do the sliders." Peter grumbles.

Back to the scene:
I'm worn out – it's been a long trip. I think I've used up every little bit of energy that God gave me. I take one last deep breath then with my head down I push through THE DOOR.

On the other side, I find a playground. Okay - not really what I would have expected. But it's great and I have it all to myself. I go to the swings – I'm a sucker for the swing. As I sit and swing, I realize I don't feel so tired anymore ; in fact, I am getting stronger. Having swung for a good long while, I run through the water feature – I always wanted to do that – they didn't have those when I was little. WHAT FUN! Maybe I shouldn't have waited to do it. Maybe I should have done it with Olivia when I had that chance.

Now the huge slide looks inviting – it looks fast with some nice curves. The landing looks soft so I don't think I'll break any of these old bones. I climb the steps to the top. When I take my place, ready to push off, I realize arms are around me. I think "Buddy, is that you?"

He responds "Who else would be with you".

I think "I thought the Angel of Death would be along this trip".

He says out loud "You know, Gwennie, you can use your outside voice. The Wiley One can't hear your voice anymore."

I think "But Buddy, I want to enjoy this last time."

"Should I use the Holy Duct Tape?"

Laughing, I think "Only if you have the pretty paisley printed kind from Miss Nipper's shop."

"If you want to just watch and talk like old times that's okay."

"Buddy, when we get to the bottom, will you leave me ?"

"NEVER"

"Back to my question, I thought the Angel of Death was assigned this duty."

"One of the joys of being ME is that I get to decide what I want to do. This was one trip I wanted to make."

"I'm glad you are here. Thanks for coming. What about everyone else back there - are they going to be okay while you are sliding with me? What if someone needs you?"

"Gwennie, you will understand later...PARTICIPATE -- DON'T ANTICIPATE, remember."

I just sit there with his arms around me for a minute.

"Gwennie, you ready."

A deep breath…

"Buddy, did we do it?"

"You mean the hints?"

"Yeah"

"Did we leave enough hints so people will figure it out ?"

"You will find out. Are you ready now?"

"Did you remember to pack my little black bag?"

"It's waiting on you at the end."

"What about the other thing we talked about ?"

"It's just like we discussed -even wrapped as you requested."

One really deep breath….

"Okay, let's go Buddy."

"One, two, three….PUSH".

"Buddy, is that Mom?"

"Yes"

"Is she pregnant with Shane? I don't remember her looking like that when we lived in Columbia."

"It's not Columbia; it's New Orleans."

"Oh, so it's Susan."

"Yes, it's Susan or as the rest of the world called her, Deborah Ann. "

"Sister. Will she be the one waiting for me at the end?"

"Nope. Are you going guess throughout this trip?"

"Of course, it's a game, isn't it?!!"

"Gwennie, you make me laugh."

"I know stupid Gwen tricks. I guess I get to keep my sense of humor. Will I have to wear white all the time? You know I love colors – Pink is nice. Maybe you could talk to someone about wearing a pale pink gown if red and hot pink are not options."

"Gwennie, are you watching?"

"I see two people that look familiar but I don't think I ever met them. Is it them?"

"Yes."

"I look like her. I have his eyes. Why didn't you stop them?"

"Free will – you know that pesky little concept."

"Yeah. Why would Ya'll have think that up? It would have saved us, little people a lot of trouble!"

"You know why – but I'll say it if you want."

Silence.

"It's the delivery room. There I am – I was cute!"

"You were precious. So tiny. Do you see me by the doctor?"

"Buddy, it's kind of gross that you were in the delivery room. "

"I think we are ready to move on. There you are at the Florida Children's Home."

"Yeah, Ya'll were showing out weren't You."

"Just a little – It's not like another parting of the Red Sea or a Virgin Birth. It's only a couple hours by car and only a state line. There weren't any border police after all."

"I love you Buddy. By the way, is everyone watching on a big TV screen or something in Heaven's main square ? I don't think I want them to see my delivery room shot not to mention when I wasn't good."

"Gwennie, the big screens are playing but everyone is watching it with loving eyes. "

"Buddy, I don't remember but did IT say 'no embarrassment' long with no more tears."

"Only in the Gwennie translation as you liked to call it! Why you insisted on combining every translation and rewriting a few to make meaning in your life - no one understands but ME."

"Of course, You did AND admit it. You loved it about me!"

"That is one of the things…yes… Are you ready to keep going?"

"I'm just participating not anticipating.   You are the driver remember…."

"I should never have given you that opening…I knew this ride would be nothing a mere angel could handle."

"I guess I'm not the only who has had the Buddy as an escort! I guess I am a handful!"

"You are more than one handful – it's been that way your whole life. Let's get going because you are going to love the end of the beginning."

"Hey, that's a song."

"Who do you think helped write it?"

"Very funny. It's playing in the background now. Boy, I hope Grey gets to the do the slide he has always wanted music playing at the Epic moments of his life. You have to do this for him. "

"I'll keep your idea in mind."

"Buddy, look – it's Daddy and me in the kitchen. It's the 'Chosen Child' story. Now I'm in the living room with Dr. Altman. Was that my salvation date ? I wondered about it because I always remember You and talking to You. I don't remember not believing and trusting Ya'll."

"Gwennie, you were saved. It doesn't matter the exact time and place. Some people like your daddy Bill and Billy Graham can remember the specific date. You are like Ruth Graham who just always understood and that's okay."

"Buddy, I was looking for a specific date; not theology."

"I know but I couldn't resist – you know that's part of my job description as well. 10/20/67. How does that sound?"

"That's my Gotcha Day."

"Yep. Let's say that We gotcha the same day your earthly family gotcha."

"I don't know about your theology there."

"Does it matter? We are after all on the right slide."

"No. It doesn't matter. Just wondered..."

"We will do a class on it later."

"Oh goody, what is the highest grade I can make in heaven ?"

"Spoken like the Magna Cum Laude you were...NEXT..."

"Wait, Buddy, who is going to be at the bottom ? St. Peter?"

"Not saying!"

"Look, it's the yellow Volkswagen bug. I was really good singer."

"Nothing like modesty."

"It's truth."

"Can we watch me do 'Half-Breed' or 'Bad, Bad Leroy Brown?"

"You forgot 'Rockin' Robin."

"Oops. That's where Scott and I thought that Hankie would make a good little lamb but he got stuck. Buddy, I think I just want to watch for a while without the commentary. Do you think you can slow it down just a little so I don't miss anything?"

"Gwennie, we will not miss a thing. "

We rode the slide for what seemed like hours. Passed all the good moments and every embarrassing moments! Sometimes I wanted to just close my eyes...but Buddy wouldn't let me. It was strangely freeing. I saw the mistakes through new eyes. I wasn't seeing a sinner – I was seeing a saint who sins occasionally - A little shout out to Dr. Neil Anderson for that one. I wish I could have seen this before The Door. Life would have been a little more fun.

"Gwennie, are you watching with your eyes open?"

I thought "Sorry, mind was wondering."

"Oh boy. That was a good line."

"So you remember 'Computers don't make mistakes. The MEN , who program them, do.'"

"Of course, it was a great. I wasn't scared of him or the fact that 'Women can't think on the same level as Men'. It was worth the B just to get that one zinger and the experience. Buddy, why does it feel like sometimes were just faster than others?"

"That's just Life, Gwen. Keep it for your little black bag."

There is Lakeland; then Danbury. It was still as cold as I remember. But what fun at the same time...I saw the trips into the city – box seats at Shea! Who would have thought it – when I watched those hours of Braves baseball that I would be see Shea stadium. Oh, there is Boston. Love it! Backed to Lakeland. Happy times and dark times there. I really didn't want to see those dark days. It was a little easier now because I saw that I survived and it really did have a purpose.

Look at the heated sidewalks at GE Plastics headquarters. What a fun place Pittsfield. Saratoga and the races were the coolest Finance Department outing ever! Especially for someone that loves the Kentucky Derby

...Southern commentary: My family calls me all day on the first Saturday in May - just in case I forget. Even been to some great Derby Parties...still looking for a box seat for a Run for the Roses, if anyone has them. Back to the story...

Tanglewood – boy...how cool. Learning to cook Wilted Spinach (Mara's recipe) which became a favorite that I fixed for the parental units.

"Buddy, will MawMaw Wilkinson be at the bottom?"

 A snort.

"It's our family trip to the beach. I painted Brayden's two toes because he wanted to be like Aunt Gwen. 'Papa watch my toes.' He was so cute! Buddy, why did they have to tell him it was girly? It was sweet – I only did the 2 toes he picked after all."

"Gwen, I can tell you why but I don't think you want to know."
"You are so right. It was just a comment – not requiring explanation."

"It's the time Papa and I took Brayden and Tucker to Natchez Trace. Sometimes I wondered if Dad remembered anything about parenting on that trip. Poor Tucker. Daddy would get him dressed and hand him off to me. He ended up in the shower every time! I will not mention the pool episode. I will leave that for his slide ride! But I am laughing as I did then...look how sweet, he is collecting candy off every cleaning cart. Cute kid that could get every cleaning lady to give him a piece. He must have collected 50 pieces. I'm just glad that he only had 2 little hands."

"Olivia. Oh, it's ARTS. I wanted to see if she inherited that Weinberg and Wilkinson artistic genes. I think she did."
"Yes, she did."
"Will she teach Madden Leigh all about ARTS?"
"You will get to see what happens when we finish the ride."

It's my talk with MawMaw Weinberg. Boy, thank Ya'll for that moment.
"We thought you needed it but she needed it as well."

"Buddy, oh Buddy, is it PawPaw and MawMaw Weinberg?"
"Nope."
"At least, I got an answer to that one."

"Buddy, I'm leaving VF. Hold tight because this part was really, really fast the first time around."

"Look it's Shane and Olivia with the Jesus Cube. What a cool thing. Thanks for letting me hear that when I was there."

"We thought you needed it then."
"You were right."

"Aren't We always!"

"Very funny."

The ride keeps going and going and going. I don't know more about the ride because it hasn't happened yet. I do know it gets really fast...like we are flying down the slide. P.S. This slide is bigger than it looked in the playground.

"Gwennie, hold tight we are going to slide right into home plate."

"Buddy, this is awesome! Who Buddy ??"

"Participate DON'T Anticipate!"

"Here we go."

"Buddy, this ride has been great – both times. Thanks for being there with me. It was so much more fun with a friend."

"Gwennie, this is when others will escort you."

Out loud I say : "Buddy, will I still be able to talk to you?"

"With your inside or outside voice, anytime...thanks for the ride."

"You going to tell me – who is waiting ??? It's your last chance."

"You know who. I don't have to tell you."

"But I want you to say it."

"Nope."

We slide through those pearly gates. Laughing. Coming to a stop, I realize Buddy's arms aren't around me anymore...I look up.

"Bubba, I knew it would be you."
"Buddy, told me to tell you – You were right all along. Now come here!"

I run into my big brothers arms. They feel like Buddy's but different.

"Bubba, it's good to see you. Thanks for getting me into THE PARTY."
"My pleasure, little sis. What kind of Oldest Brother would I be if I couldn't arrange an invitation to THE PARTY of the Centuries."

THE WALK

"Look how much you have grown since I last saw you." Bubba says has he breaks the hug to hold me at arms length.

"Bubba, if you pinch my cheeks or pat my head, I am going to think you came from Mississippi and not Bethlehem. Shouldn't you be speaking with a Bethlehem accent. Hey, are we really talking in Aramaic now – and I just think it's English with a Southern dialect?" I say using my best impression of Scarlett O'Hara.

"Gwennie, you are such a drama queen."

"You love it."

"Scarlett O'Hara you are not."

"But I can do her if I need…after all tomorrow is another day."

"Before you start overacting, I want to take you some place. I do appreciate you using the real last line instead of the more famous line."

"Frankly, my dear, I am not Rhett Butler. Now am I?! Besides, I liked that about Scarlett. If it was a bad day, there is always tomorrow…Do you want me to sing Annie now? You know I practiced that song a lot but you never let me play the role on Broadway!"

"Oh yeah, I remember. "

"Bubba, before we go, shouldn't I change?"

"What do you mean?"

"I'm still wearing my Wranglers. I mean in true "VF Imagewear Customer Service Fashion Show Guidelines" with appropriate heels, t-shirt, and cute little jacket but they are still jeans. Are Jeans allowed here ? I surely do not want to run into my mother or grandmother if I am underdressed! You know how they are."

"Gwen, I know them better than you do."

"Exactly! So you know what I'm saying. When am I getting my white robe, I asked Buddy about a color but I will try the white…but all eternity in white sounds boring…."

Bubba just laughed, took my hand, and started walking. I grabbed his hand with my other. Then I felt it. The Scar.

"Gwennie, I know you want to cry right now but no tears in heaven. It was in the King James Version…pretty specific."

"But Bubba..."

"'Did you just 'but' your big brother? The Big Brother you always wanted. "

"Yes. Should I have asked Buddy about the demerit system before I got here? You know Liberty University had these demerits – 1 for dirty room (usually it was my toothpaste on the mirror) – some for going off campus without a permission slip."

"Gwennie, I am well aware of the demerit system at Liberty. I know Jerry Falwell – Buddy helped with that dream. I also know that you never yourself got a demerit even though you should have, SCARLETT."

"Well, Bubba whatever do you mean?" I say as Scarlett.

"We saw when you skipped campus."

"You mean…"

"Yes, the time you left campus after Sunday Worship but before Sunday school."

"We were going to THOMAS ROAD for a real church service."

"Yes…and…"

"We needed a pass to get off campus."

"But did YOU, little sister, have said pass?"

"Of course not, the office was closed. We only decided we wanted to go on the way to Sunday school."

"So how did you get off campus? Was the Guard off duty?"

"Well, not exactly…."

"Did he just wave you through?"

"Well…do we really need to rehash this – you know I just saw it on The Slide…"

"How did you get off campus Gwen?"

"I drove in my car."

"Alone?"

"No. There were others in the car."

"AND….spit it out, Gwennie."

"Okay, Okay…I played Scarlett O'Hara…and before you get snippy…I turned on the tears and told him I didn't know we needed pass just to go to Thomas Road for Sunday service. The tears worked. He said 'It was okay; but next time, I would need a pass.' And I know you are going to make me say it so I'll say it… The others thought the tears were real until I started laughing as soon as my window was rolled up."

Bubba doesn't say anything so I feel a need to fill the silence.

"So are we going to spend all of eternity rehashing everyone's sins because I'm thinking that's going to be pretty boring – surely, Ya'll have something better planned !"

Bubba laughed and said "No, but we will spend it reliving some of the funny Gwen moments. "

"Gee. You know I'm not thinking I like this Big Brother relationship. I thought Buddy's job was conviction. You are just supposed to be loving and kind, selfless. By the way, I've watched enough Law and Order to recognize a prosecutor vs. a defense attorney! So who is acting now?""

"Gwennie, Good one! You know Dad and I were watching."

"Yeah right, but you know before the punishment I always had to say what I did wrong."

"For someone that could turn on the tears, real or Memorex, to get out of spankings - you have this real picture of what happened."

"Ya'll made me smart. I figured out the system really quickly."

"The beauty of heaven's system is that now we can just laugh at your acting abilities."

"I feel so much better now."

"By the way, I was standing up."

"You mean in the throne room? "

"On the right – pleading your case. So I was doing my defense attorney - but a great defense attorney has to know what his client will say. It's call client prep but I know you are been prepped for one of your jobs. So I save that teachable moment for someone who needs it."

"So how did you get me out of it?"

"Just showed him my hands…it's all it took. Of course, I couldn't help but say something – besides, now she realizes that she can act. It going to come in handy someday. My little sister needs some laughter and fun after all. They do have a lot of rules at that school. She is not used to having rules and being told what to do. We have let her be raised with a mind of her own. She pretty strict on herself and this place is not helping her. Not enough fun for her. I want her to have fun."

"And he bought it?"

"He tried to look stern but I could tell he was trying not to laugh in front of the others. He used his most booming voice to say 'You know why she is there. It's not for fun – it's for her future! She needs the training for hints.' That was just for the audience though…I know what he was thinking."

"OKAY, spill it!"

"Papa said to Me with his inside voice 'We have created a little monster but isn't she going to do great. She is getting better with her hints. I know it's hard to watch but you know that she needs to have this year. She needs to hear these speakers – she needs to have Dr. Towns for Old Testament'."

"Did you by chance ask him to let "the cup" of a certain substitute professor pass over me? Because you know he made us learn the books of the Old Testament! Dr. Towns had specifically said he was more interested in us learning the content than the order."

"I did. By the way, the son heard you. You forgot to use your inside voice!"

"Thank you dear brother for reminding me that I sometimes said things instead of thinking them! Again, "the I told you so" part of your nature did not make it into the King James Version. "

"Well, I guess it's a good thing that you read all of them – and made up your own. Never were a believer of any of that stuff were you."

"Just seemed a little ridiculous thing to worry about. After all, you weren't speaking English when the red words were written. Again, what does it matter which version someone uses ? Whether they said "Hail Mary, Full of Grace" or sing "I Surrender All"? Do they know You or do they not ? Tell me was

I right – are people surprised at who made it…is it funny to watch someone realize that people who were sprinkled are living next door?"

"I'll have to let you watch one day."

"So Cool. Bubba, where might we be going ?"

"Are you participating or anticipating?"

"I'm just wondering if I should have worn different shoes? I have on heels."

"Gwennie, you can't get blisters in heaven."

Laughing at myself, "Sorry, but it took me 40+ years to learn not to wear the same shoes 2 days in a row. It's feels like it's been years since I had on this same outfit. How long was I on the slide ? What year is it now."

"Don't know. We don't have clocks or watches. "

"Okay– so how am I supposed to be on time for Heavenly Choir Practice."

"Gwen, do you really think we would make you be in the choir after all the choir, band, piano, and handbells practices you were FORCED to attend?"

"Well, Bubba, it wasn't all bad. I liked marching band. Doing the Flag Corp kick-line was fun. Carrying the band's banner with Leigh Anne in the Apple Festival Parade was good. We even made the yearbook. I even enjoyed Mr. Stokes' stories. I guess some of it rubbed off on me because at least I can recognize a Good French Horn when I hear it! The Mission Trips were fun - especially my first to DC...even though I couldn't sing, I did get to play the bells there twice! I did get go down on the floor of the House. Right where Ronnie stood back in the good old days."

"So do you want to be musical up here?"

"I don't know. What are my other options?"

"There are a lot...but we don't have to decide right now. Okay?"

"Whatever you say - you are the perfect one. Where are we going first?"

"Home, of course."

"Oh yeah, did you finish mine ?"

"Of course!"

"Well, I was just wondering if we helped on it or something. Pick out the color scheme and flooring. You know I have experience with building Habitat homes."

"Surely, Gwennie, you are not thinking that Safety Coordinator and Water girl duties qualify you as a Construction Supervisor."

"Hello, I have my own hard hat complete with my name on it! I did hammer, paint, and clean on each house. You know I'm a GREAT Safety Coordinator. I had to be!"

"One nail and ½ the ceiling…plus the Tom Sawyer act on the first house doesn't really mean you built it."

"Hey, Hey…are you saying that my nail and ½ the ceiling were not critical because they were. And just because the SOS keep trying to instruct me on the proper way to paint a base coat on the baseboard…wasn't my fault. Hello, they do say unskilled labor – and that's what they got – but I can't turn off my mind. He had to show me again and again - I only need one demonstration. When he had finished the multiple demonstrations. There was only a yard left. Besides he was already bent over and had the paint brush. It didn't make sense for me to do get more paint on me. It's called 'Process Improvement'. "

"Right - another of those times. I concede that you were a GREAT Safety Coordinator. You protected a couple of key people that day - even if a really cute Supervisor was on the roof of the next house."

"Hey, I'm human - you should understand that it wasn't like I was lusting...I was just admiring! So it was the same as the crying for the guard?"

"Almost, but you know the best Habitat story would be 'Volunteer Meeting at the Fellowship Building.'"

Laughing, I say "You mean when I pulled out Scarlett on the co-coordinator of the Build."

"Yep."

"They were getting nowhere and it was taking forever. I was bored and we had people that didn't need to hear more stories. They were promised a short meeting! You know I didn't realize I did Scarlett until Lisa said something to me after the meeting."

"Yep."

"Ya'll wanted me to realize it – that I was using my Southern charm – funny , yes – effective, yes but only in the short term. Oops! I missed a hint opportunity there."

"Yeah you did but We fixed it later."

"Thanks for catching it. I did try to reframe from doing it as much after that….only pulled it out when the people wouldn't respond to me as anything else but damsel in distress. You have to admit that I would have eventually had to use it at the

Volunteer Meeting - it was the only way someone would hear me."

"I know. You were a quick study. Only a few lessons did you need repeating."

"I can think of one now. I truly was sick of learning that lesson."

"We were truly sick of having you struggle through it as well. Luckily, for you, laughter was always involved. You can make even dealing with auditors fun!"

"Did I have a choice? It said I had to rejoice in all circumstances. It was easier to make it a game – try to beat them before they got something."

"I think that other RedKap'ers picked up on it."

"They probably gave me the idea. Hey, Jesus."

"Yes. Where are the others?"

"What do you mean?"

"I mean I thought more people would be on the streets of Gold. There aren't any people on the road. Is it mandatory Chapel Day? Heavenly Choir practice?

"Gwen, there are people all around us. You even know some. They are trying to get your attention."

"Well, I'm just going to have to add it to my little black bag – because I'm not seeing them."

"No need for the black bag. Your eyes haven't adjusted yet. Haven't you noticed that it's bright?"

"Yes. In fact, I was thinking I would have a migraine before The Door."

"It's just something We do for new arrivals. It helps them transition and rest."

"Bubba, do you mean "Be Still and Know" ?

"You are just so funny! What happened to Jesus? The show of proper respect to your eldest brother."

"Well, it's like when someone called me, Gwendolyn Leigh"

"I think Gwendolyn Leigh you are remembering Scott's childhood not your own."

"I wasn't remembering anyone's childhood just using an example. Besides, it's not polite to use someone else's name when making a negative comment – unless you add 'Bless their little heart'. "

"Gwennie, you're not in Tennessee anymore."

" Wait a Minute…you mean that TN is not heaven. I thought it was. Really, Nashville is a really cool place – it's reminded me of Home – I promise….it has mountains and nature, historical sites, big city stuff like the Symphony Hall. Do you remember Hayden singing there? I can't wait to see where else he sings! But, yes, I know I'm not supposed to use that word, the best part about Nashville is her people. It's like a small town because everyone knows everyone - REALLY the whole state is like that. You know I have known generous, giving people in my life. I have never seen so many of them in one place. It's not hard to find Jesus eyes. It's still a place where Wednesday Night is Church night – at least part of the year. I promise."

"Was that commercial sponsored by the Governor's Commerce Commission?"

"Well, I had already plugged VF earlier – so I thought I would get in Nashville now."

Bubba had to stop at that point because he was laughing to hard to continue walking.

FROM GLW to READER : Okay, I was really laughing out loud as I wrote that so I had to stop typing...now I'm back…

"Seriously, thanks for explaining the no people thing. I mean I love Ya'll but I promised some people I would look them up when I got here – and then I promised those back behind The

Door, I would check on their people if I reached Home before them."

"Gwennie, sweetie, don't worry we know how much you love to talk to strangers – we will have enough people so you can meet a new person every day and still have some left over."

"Well, I don't think that's going to work either. I am going to have to meet more than 1 per day – exactly what should my daily target be so I can meet everyone?"

Bubba is shaking his head. He raises my hand to his lips.

"What are you thinking ? Remember I can't read your mind Bubba!"

"I'm thinking that you want to be Heaven's WalMart Greeter."

"Well, I do have experience and if you can just ask Uncle Jimmy, he will give me a reference. "

"I am aware that your first job was part-time receptionist for Boswell Oil Company, Meridian MS."

"So you know that I was really good."

"Yes you were exceptional for a 5-year old. You were also good at greeting people at Baptist's ICU ward while your earthly daddy, Bill, had open heart surgery."

"Buddy knew I needed something to do or I would break down. I had to stay in Dartha Sr. character and focused on others until Mom made it to town."

"Yes, We taught you that trick. Being able to act like someone else when you were emotionally or spiritually overloaded. "

"Well, thanks. It was really Buddy – he would just prompt me with the name during those times."

"I know sweetie. You had to fake the smile sometimes before it turned real. That's okay – you got better and faster at it each time. Just remember I think you were the best."

"I'm not sure why Ya'll find it so amusing. You were the ones that created me to work in opposing quadrants. Analytical and Creative. I know it's weird – I heard that all my adult life – after I was comfortable in my own skin. The people from my teenage years probably wouldn't think so because they didn't see the real me. They saw me trying to be You."

"Gwennie, some people did see the real you. Should I mention a box of shotgun shells or a Magnum P.I. tee shirt? I was so proud of you when you decided to forgive the hurts Bill had to endure. You know it was his pain but it was part of all of your journey. We needed you to experience it or you wouldn't have gone where we needed. Really, how else were we going to get a

Southern Baptist Christian Ed Lay Leader to Hermitage United Methodist Church?"

"Well, I didn't think YOU would resort to trickery. I mean you used poor little Claudia in your scheme. Was that really nice?"

"Gwennie, we tried having her just inviting you to the Singles class and other events."

"Bubba, you know how I feel about Singles classes. I don't have to remind you about the times I've been involved in the Singles ministry. You know about the situations. And I emphasis the "s" – multiple times!"

"Again, couldn't help it."

"Well, you could at least stop laughing now. It wasn't funny then."

"Oh but it was!"

"Bubba, again, the KJV did not mention this teasing aspect of your nature."

"Really Gwennie, we thought that Cousin Michael and the many other "temporary big brothers" would have taught you that your Eldest brother enjoys to tease you?"

"Well, really you didn't have to go so far. I would have thought Papa would have stopped you."

"He wants me to have fun as well."

"Am all for fun but let's see if we can't find you someone else to tease for all of eternity!"

"Can I tease you just a little – maybe every other day – oh I forgot – no clocks…that idea is out." He laughs.

"I think we should just continue this journey in silence for a while. Besides, I want to focus on trying to get my Heaven eyes."

"Gwen, you really can't make yourself be ready."

"I could try. Besides, if you tell me I can't, it will just make me try harder."

"Then I'll just be quiet." Bubba finally relents. It's really hard for him not to be Rabbi, Teacher - that part is in the KJV!

We continue following the golden street. Of course, this image leads my thoughts to The Wizard of Oz. I am just contemplating if is it proper Heaven behavior to sing Movie tunes and do the little dance...When Bubba starts whistling the song - It takes less than a second for me to start whistling (GLW: I'm a much better whistler in Heaven) and we start to do the little dance.

"So Bubba, which version did you like Best: The one with Judy Garland, The Wiz with Diana Ross and Michael Jackson, or Wicked?"

"You first."

"You already know I liked Wicked best! It was the back story - the WHY - but not sure I would have liked the book. I heard it was darker than the musical. I had enough dark during real life - I liked happy endings for entertainment. So your turn?"

"No comment." Then He winked and I heard the answer from His inside voice.

GLW: Can't tell you if you really want to know...add it to your little black bag!

I wink back "I got it. You can't really show favorites. I'll try not to tell people that I am your favorite!"

"Gwen, it's more like you are all my favorites."

"I'm not sure that's what I want to hear. Bubba, this isn't just a visit remember - I'm staying FOR A LONG TIME. Let's take it easy on explaining every mystery of the universe today. Besides, I'm getting tired. I think the KJV was specific about mounting up on the wings of eagles."

"Do I need to sprout wings?"

I sigh heavily.

"Okay, Scarlett, we are almost there. Can you see the mountains over there?"

"It is TN- see I told you!"

"Not really, but..."

"Bubba, please don't burst my bubble. It is already starting to feel more like Home. Besides, were Ya'll the ones that kept sending message for me to 'Be Still and Know'? Please tell me I don't have to be still all of eternity."

"Please address me as Rabbi if you want an answer." Bubba tried to use his stern teacher voice but it didn't scare me.

"I didn't use Rabbi the first time, did I? Nope...I already know the answer...figured it out."

"What makes you so sure."

"Well, for one Your wink used your whole face. "

I figured out that I can't type everything about this trip.

"Told Buddy he didn't need to worry."

"Very funny, Buddy worry. Remember I've been with him for the last 40+ years."

We continue on...just swinging our joined hands as we do. Occasionally, we whistle a few more shared favorite songs. Some a little require a little dancing or raised hands. GLW: I hope that doesn't shock some High Church folks.

"Are we almost there?"

"Are you ready, Gwennie?"

"You know me. Have I ever not taken a shower after a trip ? Let me tell you this has been one long trip, Brother Dear."

"Okay."

"Oh, it's pretty."

"Is it what you thought it would be?"

"No, not really."

"Do you recognize it?"

"It's not the one of the river. It's the Car Dealership Home."

"Better?"

"Yes. It's definitely beats the one I would I have picked. Much better."

"I thought this would work best for you given your responsibilities."

"Oh goody, I get a job. What is it?"

"Participate DON'T Anticipate."

"Boy, do you ever get tired of the Rabbi role?"

"Yeah, that's why I revert back to Big Brother mode."

"I hope we work out an even balance soon. Or I'm going to need a nap. You are quicker than I am."

"Yep...I had to be Perfect. You just had to be the Best!"

"I think that I have heard that somewhere."

"Remember Buddy is the creative one. I'm sure he would have created a game or some problem to occupy you."

"He didn't forget my sukodo books, did he?"

"Why, is your mind racing?"

"No. I just wondered if I get to do Sukodo."

"Gwen, would you like to go inside ?"

"I was kind of waiting. Something about a bridegroom to the church. Me being part of said church and a threshold...I thought since it was my dream but better I would just 'Participate'."

Bubba did pick me up...only to throw me over his shoulder.

"Very Funny!"

"I'm just a simple carpenter remember. Buddy would have done it your way...but I'm not Buddy."

"Yeah, I am starting to realize that. But couldn't Ya'll have talked about it before hand."

"Do you really want to go there?"

I decide that silence isn't a bad thing since I'm still hanging over his shoulder...so he kicks open the door. Once inside, he does sit me down on my feet facing inside. I take a few steps inside the foyer. Just like I had told Buddy, there is a round table under a large chandelier which hangs from a vaulted ceiling. I walk over to it. Typically, I would have placed fresh flowers in a large crystal vase on such a table. But Buddy had out done himself! It was just like we talked about with our inside voices!

Bubba is still standing by the door.

"So Bubba did you peek?"

"Was I told not to peek?"

"Yes. I know, I know you are the perfect one. I just tried to played one in the real life. Come look."

He walks up to the table. It a stack of presents all wrapped in different shades of pink with coordinating bows. Martha Stewart would be so proud. It is just perfect. So Gwennie. I look at a few of the tags to find the one I want.

"Buddy and I had this idea. To answer my black bag questions, You and I could "do lunches"...for every lunches, we have a different present."

"Do you want to open it?"

"Not yet. I'm just participating now."

"It's okay Bubba - remember no tears. Besides, I'm not really sure I want to see tears of blood."

Bubba laughs "Way to lighten the mood."

"Told you I saw too much darkness in real life. I get happy and light now. KJV promised and Buddy told me that part was dead on accurate!"

When he doesn't start to open it, I decide to tell him the other part of our surprise. I look around for the second gift. It takes a few minutes for me to find it. Maybe we should have numbered these as part of the plan ? Oh well...here it is.

"I did say 'Let's do lunch'...but we thought of this cool way to do it. I know you love teachable moments but I know you love people's stories more. Just like me! So...our idea was to have you bring a guest or two when you feel like the time is right. We thought you might want to invite your Mom to the second one." I hand him the second package and take the first so he can read the card.

"Okay, You have got to open read the tag now because it's killing me!"

He does and a smile grows on his face. I can tell from his eyes that he likes the idea.

"So...remember I can't read Your thoughts!"

Bubba says "To Mom...From Jesus. That is good."

"We knew you would love this part. Plus this is so much more my style than the laying them at your feet thing. So not special enough."

Bubba places his mom's package back in the exact place so as to keep the stack symmetrical. I can tell this is going to be hard living with someone who really is perfect. It give me new appreciation for the gift of singleness!"

"Gwennie, I don't really live in the house with you."

"I know but could you please restrain yourself with reading my thoughts."

"Buddy got to read them all."

"That's his job - a Big Brother should not know all the little sister's secrets...at least not until she tells him - when sufficient time has elapsed."

"Okay - you would think that you were the first little sister I had."

"I'm not and I will not be the last. But I am the first Gwendolyn Leigh Wilkinson little sister...the one and only."

"I can assure you that we did not create two of you."

"Oh goody, so one black bag question is gone."

"Gwen, did you think that you had a twin?"

"Well, Cotton talk to someone who looked enough like me that it wasn't until she spoke did he realize it wasn't me. And lately, it was all the Sarah Palin look alike stuff. Really, was it necessary for the have a man stop 4 times to see if I was her? To think that Sarah come to FBC Lenoir City after the Nashville Tea Party! Please...it was over kill!"

"That wasn't my idea - that was Buddy...but I loved it! If you hand over my present, I'll go fix lunch - as we have to "do lunch"...while you go upsides and take that shower you wanted."

I draw it closer to me. " You can't open it until I get back. Hey, you mean we have bathrooms in Heaven."

"Gwennie, I thought Angy Morrison covered where God is...we lived in the bathroom remember."

I can only laugh. Some of my best ideas came when I was blow drying my hair each morning...so I knew Buddy was in there.

"Okay, I'm just going to be nosy and find my bathroom."

"Quit trying to picture it...just go!"

As I head of the stairs, I have to think it's really good. It is so me. Bubba yells from below...

"Gwennie, I think you will like what We left for you to wear for lunch."

Okay, so now I'm walk just a little faster. In fact, I'm excited. Please let it be not a white flowing gown!

There it is!

My favorite red dress...I love the A line cut! I stop in my tracks...are those what I think they are? I slowly approach because I am scared they might disappear. I think perhaps I should just touch them. Yep, I feel them! Do I dare to look inside??

From downstairs, I hear "Gwen, do really think they are fakes?"

I yell back. "I don't know. I've only seen them on TV! By the way, is there any 'tripping downstairs while wearing the highest heels ever made' allowed in Heaven?"

"I'm getting hungry!"

"Bubba, relax - I'm coming."

I don't even really explore the bathroom. I will do that after lunch since he so hungry! Really, thinking the big brother image was maybe not what I thought it would be...but I do have Jimmy Choo's so I guess it's going have its advantages!

Okay, that feels better. I wonder if there is something else. To the right a mirror. Oh yeah. The Red Dress and the perfect shoes...I need a bracelet though...when He doesn't yell up the answer. I do a little looking around...there it is. Perfect. Black. Couldn't find the Black Pocketbook - so I guess I'll have to find it later. We will just make due for first lunch and learn!!!

I take a few steps testing the shoes. Hey, I can walk in these but I better take it slow on the stairs. I'm only have way down the stairs when Bubba steps around the corner and says "it's about time."

"I was right on time. Thank you."

"Again, I so appreciate the Southern Etiquette lesson."

"Well, I'm just trying to help. You were born in a different time."

"You forget that I've seen it all."

"Yeah, but I can't stop being me."

"Gwennie, I thought we would eat in the sun room."

"I love it. Just right."

"Only just right???"

I sigh then say with exaggerated excitement (which is hard given that I really am tired). "It's just PERFECT."

"Much better. I like A GREAT DEAL of positive encouragement - I just don't NEED it like some I know."

"Again, thank you for that teachable moment, Rabbi." He holds out the chair so I sit. Then he joins me.

"So I now know that Mary raised you right and I don't have to give you Southern Charm lessons."

"Who in the world do you think taught it to the first Southern Gentleman?"

"Buddy."

"Gwennie, you are just too fun. I know he isn't your favorite."

"But who is my favorite?"

"I the Perfect One already know the answer."

"One Point, Bubba. Since I just started keeping score, I'll give myself a 0. Like a little Handicap. Does that sound fair and just ?"

"Wait, you think you can win against MR. PERFECT!"

"You forget Mr. PERFECT...Buddy, had me all to himself for 40+ years! I have been trained by THE BEST."

"Okay, little sis you are on."

"Mr. PERFECT, are you sure you can take me after all didn't Kathy and I win our first ever hand of ROOK against Butch and Kenneth?"

"Yes and you never played another hand."

"That's because they wouldn't play. Besides have you forgotten that I can win poker even when I tell people my hand."

"Oh yeah, I also remember who taught you to play poker...and how 2 others wanted to play strip poker?"

"Yep, but a Marine, who was older, said no but still taught me to play!"

"You were always a sucker for a uniform!"

"If you say so..."

"Oh but I do know you best!"

"Okay, Mr. Perfect, May we say grace so I can begin?"

"Gwennie, do you need my help or do you want to try it yourself?"

"I can do it MYSELF, MR. Perfect. Bubba who is winning."

"Gwennie, I think we tied but it's only first few minutes of the game."

"Bow your head Bubba." I reach for his hand. Pause for a few seconds. Then say a prayer worthy of my 1st Graders. Simple. Straight from the heart. And oh so honest!

"I can't believe that Buddy taught you to pray through first graders."

"You mean pray with my outside voice right?"

"Oh, and little sis pulls ahead...but your dear friend Linda had a little part in it as well."

"Yeah, I just love the way she prays! So I will be generous and not count that point in my favor."

"Rabbi, I would love to continue this game with my ELDEST brother but it's an opportunity for a teachable moment. Now remember Bubba, how Buddy taught me - I learn best from stories or puzzles. Are you ready?"

"Gwen, you really need to eat so I will tell you a story in exchange for you eating. Do you need your little black bag for your question?"

"Bubba, you know me! The SLIDE AND The WALK didn't have beverage service, this is true - BUT Ya'll did entertain me with song. Plus you smiled when slide into home plate. You know am I sucker for a great smile especially when it reaches the eyes. "

"Gwennie, I appreciate your shout out to your favorite airline but you really do need to eat. Do you want your little black bag?"

"No need I know my first question. What is your earliest childhood memory?"

"That's it??? That's the best question you could come up with?"

"Yes, it's PERFECT shall we say."

"Okay, but you have to stop typing...."

One question led to another and another. Some really good stuff. Can't wait until you get here so you can have You can ask for yourself. It's his story so I can't really tell it. He has to tell it! I promise it's worth the wait! Besides, I did eat - and it was wonderful but I couldn't tell you what I ate...It didn't matter. It was all about the STORIES. However, I do remember dessert. Chocolate Mousse! It was first story he asked me to tell with as many words and side stories as possible. I couldn't believe it he had a black bag full of questions for me! I get to tell all my stories to a willing audience! This Eternity thing is getting better and better. I can even repeat myself because he already show it - he just wants get excited. I really should have been on stage! I'm adding another question to my black bag - "Why couldn't I go to Broadway?"

"Bubba, since you cooked, I'll do the dishes."

"Gwen, do you really think that we cook and wash dishes by hand here?"

"I think that if I want to wash dishes by hand to thank you for a meal that I didn't have to fix myself - you should let me. After all, do you know how many times I had to fix the meal and do the dishes!!!"

"Yes, I know it was hard to do what we asked and still get the rest, exercise, and food you needed. We asked a great deal of you. I hated to see you so tired."

"Bubba, no tears remember - I don't do blood! Besides, since you couldn't control that teachable moment RABBI get to dry!"

We just worked side by side for a while. Me washing and him drying. Finally someone to reach the highest shelf. No step stool needed. Another Single Girl's tool I will not be needing! This is going to be fun to tick off that list my mom and I created. I had already learned how to hang pictures by myself - except for the heavy Art pieces...so let's see how long that takes to get rid of that list.

"Gwennie, why don't we watch the sunset from the back deck? I installed this great swing for you."

"Bubba, did you want all my dates?"

"Yes. A Big Brother has to do some spying to ensure that his sister's date is sufficiently intimated!"

"Bubba, between you and Buddy plus the scores of other 'temporary big brothers' I had - it's a wonder I had any dates!"

"I know WE were really good."

"STOP LAUGHING IT'S NOT FUNNY!" with my hands on my hips and my best little sister mad face.

"Yes it is I can tell my your eyes. Go ahead let go. It's not disrespect or mean to laugh stuff like that."

So I almost let loose...it was be best laugh had ever had. No worry...here everyone is in on the joke. They get my dry wit - not intending to be mean...Oh it felt so good. I had to restrain myself for so long - No I really am feeling rested...maybe I don't have sleep up here...cool...more try new stuff...the possibilities are limitless.

"Bubba, do I have time to refreshed up?"

"Yes, you can explore the bathroom if you want."

" I just need to brush my teeth."

"Yet, right. Okay. I'll be waiting on the swing." He sighed heavily and started to walk out the door.

"I'll be back in a bit. Don't forget to take your present." I called as I slowly walked up the stairs with a grin on my face.

I enter the bathroom and close the door. I find the toothbrush and toothpaste. As I am brushing my teeth, I think 'Buddy, how am I doing?'...

He answers his outside voice "Great. Keep it up you are almost there. You know what's next...just relax and let him do it."

I think "Thanks, I had You plus some great teachers along the way. I hope they know."

He says with his outside voice, "Some do and some will know."

I say out loud. It's better than my best dream for myself.

"TOLD YOU SO!"

"Okay, does this mean that you will as tease me for eternity?"

"Participate DON'T Anticipate."

"Can I joyfully anticipate ?"

"You mean dream better dreams to see if we can out do them? Gwennie, We covered the who loves you Best part?"

"We did. Thanks, Buddy."

"You were worth it. You did what you set out to do."

"Thanks for your help. I couldn't have done it without you."

"Buddy, is this the last time?"

"NO TEARS. Do you know how large a warehouse we had to build to keep your jars?"

"No, but you know I like touring Warehouses and Plants."

Laughing Buddy replies, "Gwennie, don't worry it's already scheduled and you can be as nosy as you like! You don't have to do the hints for ME!"

"Buddy, remember the audience!"

"Touche. I did teach you well!"

"If not, Miss Linda will catch in editing. I should have know that she was going to make that dream come true."

"Yep. One of the last things you had to figure out. Are you resting now ? Do you think you can beat him?"

"You tell me."

"You are so ready. You have been STILL enough. You are a diet coke that has been shaken up!"

" Just as if Pastor D was born in Mobile, AL. See you later."

I slowly walk down the stairs. The house really better than I expected. I just remember I didn't look around the bathroom. I was too focused on Buddy! I am going to have to remember it! Next time! I can't wait to explore it! I have to get going - I am racing against a clock now. How I made it down the stairs in the shoes with my focus elsewhere...I can already tell that this place is great for a girl that trips going up the stairs. I remember having to get that accident report signed. I can't wait until that "Lunch and Learn".

I'm at the door leading out to the back deck. One deep breath...okay, I'm ready.

"Gwennie, I thought you might want to meet someone."

"Papa."

He just opened his arms. I thought "HOME, Finally."

Buddy using his inside voice says "See you were right."

Using my outside voice, I say "BUDDY, LET ME ENJOY THIS POINT JUST WITH PAPA. Participate not Anticipate...remember!"

Using my inside voice, "So Papa, how are Buddy and I doing?"

Papa whispers in my ear..."PERFECT!"

"Dad, tell Buddy that he had her for 40 yrs - It's my turn. I get to be the Teacher who unlocks the mysteries. He had his turn!"

"Papa, you really did mean it! The KJV got this Jealous God right!"

THE PORCH

In his outside voice, Papa just chuckled and said, "Look at the swing that Jesus built with his own hands."

"Papa, You are so clever. It's Gwennie size."

"Sis, I only have to measure once."

"Bubba, I know - that's why Papa is clever."

"Now, can I tell her?"

"Son, let her enjoy the sunset and the swing. Gwennie did you notice the cushions ?"

"Of course, black and white toile print with Red accents. It's perfect."

"Buddy suggested those."

We sat on the newly built swing with Papa on one side and Bubba on the other. It was like a Gwennie Size Moon Pie (let's say).

"Gwen, we are not like a moon pie. Are we drinking RC ? No, it's iced tea." Bubba remarks as he passes out the tea glasses.

"Bubba, yummy. It tastes just right - 1/2 sweet and 1/2 unsweet...complete with mint leaves! Nice touch. However, it's not nice to listen to my inside voice."

"It's a hard habit to break."

"Papa, perhaps you could get Bubba to stop reading my thoughts."

"Son, remember Participate not Anticipate."

Bubba reluctantly sits back in the swing. He puts his feet up on the table. I want to do the same, but I will take off my pretty shoes first.

"I guess I should have taken time to do my toes before I decided to take my shoes off."

"Gwennie, all you have to do here is think about the red color on your toes and it happens."

"Bubba, I know you are a guy but the fun of the pedicure is the actual work. It makes toes and feet feel great. It's better than a massage for tired muscles. It's a great Sabbath exercise. So I'm hoping that we have really good pedicure sets here."

"Gwennie, I don't go around washing feet all day long. It's not like the Golden streets are dusty."

"Bubba, where is your present? Why don't you open it ? I want Papa to see your face."

Bubba slowly unties the bow and starts to slowly unwrapped as if to save the paper.

"Bubba, you don't have to save ribbons and paper here."

"Sis, what if I want to ?"

"Then I will come up with an art project to incorporate every one of them. It might take a while. Would you like that?"

"Yes, Gwen. I would really like that."

"Will you hang it on your refrigerator with a magnet?"

"No, I have just the place to hang it."

Another Single Girl needs to be marked off the list! Bubba can hang heavy art pieces. Okay...I forgot how long the "What we need men for" list that Mom and I during my many relocations...I guess I'll remember them as I hear them.

"Papa, you made a pretty sunset tonight. Can I rest my head in your shoulder? I am really tired. When will I get over this fainting feeling? I'm ready for some fun."

"Scarlett, it's nice of you to join us tonight." Bubba says with a smirk.

"Oh are we back on the game? I thought you were opening a present."

Bubba returns to slowly, slowly opening the present. It's about to kill me! Finally, he lifts the lid! Oh the look on his face was so worth it!!

"Gwennie, a sukudo book?"

"Let's face it. A crown doesn't go with my imagine of a carpenter. So last season! What can you do w/ a crown any way ? I figured you already had more than enough of those. Besides, the puzzles helped me quiet my racing thoughts and relax after a long day. "

"Okay, so I get the Sudoku book. But why a ball point pen instead of a pencil?"

"Bubba, a pen because you are the only one that just has to measure once! The rest of us measure twice then cut once."

"Very funny. What if I get stuck?"

"Buddy and I left the clues in the back. It's meant for relaxation, not torment. If you can't think of the solution, just flip and get a hint from the back. So do you like it ?"

"Sis, you are original. Yes, I do like it. It makes me wonder about the other packages."

"You are going to love them. Remember you promised not to peek. You will enjoy seeing the gift for the first time when the other person opens it. It's going to be good. Buddy and I really thought about these gifts."

We sit quietly as Bubba works his new puzzle book. He is flying through them. It's good that Buddy rigged the present so that as he finishes on puzzle; a new one is added to the back. Good one Buddy! I'll have to figure out that magic trick later.

The sun is still setting when I say to Papa with my inside voice. "Is he distracted enough?"

"Yes, Gwennie. He isn't paying attention."

"So, can we split the screen and play the Game on the other side? You know I want to see the coin toss kick-off."

We have picture-within-picture on the ultimate wide screen. The sunset remains but Super Bowl 2010 from Miami, FL appears. What I hard day for Southerns. Do we pull for Peyton or for the Saints? For a while, it looks like it's going to be the Colts and Peyton will dominate. Suddenly, it's the half-time and the score is now tied. It's time for the half-time show. Yippee. Just like I wanted to see it! I wanted to watch the light show without the camera shots of an aging Rock Group. The background music isn't from The Who but Gloria Gainer's "I will survive" and the theme from Rocky - the original.

"Papa, who do you want to win this one ?"

"Gwennie, I can't play favorites; however, I am partial to the name Saints."

"Thought so. Is my big brother even paying attention?"

"Yes, but the Sudoku is working its magic in that he is one too many things to monitor. He still thinks you are only watching the longest sunset in history."

"How long do I play this game?"

"Let's play a little longer. Just so he can have a little rest and some fun."

"In that case, can we see the beginning of The Game? You know the scene I want - it looks like the stadium Max Lucado describes in Running with the Giants."

Instead of the sunset, a video starts. The picture is a huge baseball stadium crowded with people. While it appears like Black are one team's colors. I don't recognize the stadium from any sporting event my dad has made me watch. I can tell the Black Team are the visiting team from the scoreboard. The White Team is the home team.

At the top of the 7th inning, the Whites lead 1-0. Blacks have a runner on first and a batter up at the plate.

Wow, that pitch was close. Apparently, the Whites pitcher didn't care for the Black's batter crowding the plate. The batter isn't hit but he does moved back a few inches. That would be strike 1 and the runner has a huge lead off 1st. There is cheering from the stands, but the opponents do not like it.

Again, the batter steps in close. This time the pitcher sends a ball over to the first baseman. The runner makes it back to the base safely. However, he isn't going to be taking such a large lead toward 2nd now. The pitcher returns his attention to the batter. The batter appears to have forgotten that the Whites pitcher didn't like him crowding the plate. Again, a strike is called as the ball sails perfectly over the plate.

The Blacks are getting loud and abusive with the umpire. The umpire gives the team and its coach a warning.

The batter steps into the box but doesn't crowd. The pitch again is right in the strike zone. Oh no, I remember that swing. I've seen it a few times watching baseball throughout my life.

"Bubba, what's the score ?"

"It's still tied - remember it's just halftime."

"No, Bubba, what is the score for Blacks vs. Whites?"

He looks up from the Sudoku with narrowed eyes. Saying w/ his eyes that he knows I'm up to something. But he refuses to satisfy me, so I just have to prod a little more.

"Bubba, I like your Wranglers and the Timberland are very appropriate for a carpenter."

Now it looks like he is trying not to laugh...he is almost going to say something when I get one more Rabbi.

"Bubba, I would realize those eyes anywhere! Before you ask RABBI, I know the answer, but I'm not going to tell you. I want to see how Ya'll work it out."

"Dad, how long has she known? "

"Does it matter, Son?"

"Bubba, admit it so we can rewind the Superbowl. I want to see the halftime show lights set to my favorite music. Then I didn't get to watch the second half! I had a headache remember. Besides, I have to see who is going to Disneyworld!"

"Okay, Game. Set. to the little sister."

"Thanks to a little help from Papa and Buddy! Do you like your gift?"

"Sukodo with a pen???"

"Yes, it should occupy your mind so I can watch the game in peace...I want to savor it."

"Why?"

"It's not every day the Saints win."

Papa and I are laughing out loud at this point. Bubba decides to join in but still wants to do when I know.

"Son, let's just say 10/20/1967, because we knew she would pull this one when she was born! Look at her - she isn't perfect, but she is her best!"

"Gwennie, the Whites are head 1-0" chimes Bubba.

"Thanks, Papa. Don't we have work to be done before the game ends?"

"Nope. Already handled, I know how the game ends."

Bubba starts whistling, while doing a puzzle, 'Take me out to the ballgame'. It is after all it's the 7th inning stretch! That was probably a point for Bubba, so I start to sing it doing the conducting like Harry Carey did for so many years.

"Papa, now can we get started. We have work to do - we have 2 more innings."

"Sweetie, remember this is our sabbath - we have it covered. In fact, we are going to have a few friends will be visiting the next few days. Why don't you find your bedroom?"

THE SECOND DINNER

My eyes open - yep, it's still the same room I remember. I touch the satin comforter....the soft cotton sheets. It's real -....I pinch my arm just for good measure....no pain - kind of a tickle.

I laugh out loud. "Buddy, should have been reading my thoughts on that one."

"Who said I wasn't?"

"Buddy, it was real...not a dream!"

"Of course, what did you think?"

"It was just too perfect, like I'd done it before."

"You had. Remember the slide."

"No, I mean the Walk with Jesus and watching the game with Papa."

"You will get it - it's still just day 2 of eternity."

"Buddy, I have to go. I think I'm going to work today."

"Get OUT OF THE BED...we have WORK DO TO, little buddy."

"See ya' later....I'm getting up right now. Besides, I need to ensure that bathroom was a great as I remember!"

So I slowly slide out of that comfy bed. I remember that Bubba promised my first lunch today! I can't wait to see who it is! I love surprises.

It feels funny not doing my 30 min walk while I meditate and pray so I sing some praise songs. Amazing that I can remember the words without Youtube but again Bevy once posted that it's the same line 7 times!

I head down stairs. I start with breakfast. I don't really remember the food. It was great, but does it matter that you can eat whatever you want and not worry about weight or cholesterol? I enjoy it because it's heaven, but it's not very important anymore. I'm not thinking about it like I did before The Door.

I start my search of the house. I still can't locate my black bag. When I was studying and couldn't find the answer to something or Buddy wasn't revealing it, it was not nice that I would email Reverend Bob. Reverend Bob, a retired Methodist Ministry and Missionary belonged to HUMC with me. He sometimes could answer my questions or point me in the right direction. Other times, he would tell me to pack them into my little black bag to I could ask them when I reached Heaven. Buddy told me on the Slide that my black bag was waiting for me. I still hadn't seen it.

With a guest arriving for lunch, I knew it would be someone who related to my questions. I wanted to find the questions so I wouldn't forget!

I looked every place.

Then I started to really notice the rooms. It really had been designed with me in mind. I was prepared for myself by the Master Carpenter. I saw the little touches that only He could have know.

The little black bag forgotten.

I just wondered around the rooms. I found the music room. The baby grand piano. I sat down and tried a few notes. Oh boy! No more Tuning needed in Heaven. I started playing a few songs - not from music sheets - finally I could play from memory.   After a while, I caught myself - it's got to me almost time for lunch. I need to run up to the bathroom and freshen up before my guests.

I run up stairs and change into a dress. I don't know who is coming and do not wish to offend them.   As I am walking down the stairs, the doorbell rings. I opened it, and Bubba was there with two other people.

"Please come in. Welcome." I saw to Bubba and these two people I don't recognize.

"Gwennie, I want to introduce you to the people who raised me on earth."

"Pleased to meet you."

Of course, the first thing that enters my mind is I only know their first names. What am I supposed to call them? I am a properly brought-up Southern young lady who would not address a new person by their first names!

Bubba reading my thoughts says "Mary and Joseph are fine."

Okay, still not sure about this reading my thoughts and answering out loud.

"We have been reading your thoughts your whole life."

"Not to correct the perfect one, but I thought it might be rude in front of our guests."

Mary speaks "Gwennie, we raised him. We know he can read thoughts."

"Well, Miss Mary, I guess people in Heaven can't offense. Plus I think you just answered a question even though I couldn't find my black bag. Bubba, Miss Mary, and Mr. Joseph, please come this way. Lunch is being served in the sun room. "

"Honey, why does she refer to it as Miss and Mr. ?"

"Mom, it's a southern thing - I'll explain later."

We sit at the table preparing for us.

"Miss Mary and Mr. Joseph, I thought I might introduce you to some foods from my home. If you don't like them, we can fix something that you like better. We have sweet tea to drink, and the house "wine" is from my home. In this dish we have Chicken 'N Dumplings with the fixins as we call them. Enjoy. "

Bubba chuckles at my explanation.

I ask a little about their experience here. We exchange pleasantries.   After a few minutes, Bubba reminds me about my questions.

"We were told as children that when you met your cousin Elizabeth when you were pregnant that her Baby (John the Baptist) leapt in her womb.[Luke 1:41] Did anything else like that happen while you were pregnant? Pregnant women are supposed to glow. Did people think you had an extra glow?"

Miss Mary just laughed and asked Mr. Joseph about the extra glow part.

"Okay, Miss Mary when Jesus was a baby, how did you know when to feed him? I mean the babies I was around cried when they wanted to be fed and then when it wasn't forth coming they screamed. The song we sang at Christmas says "No sound did he make!" The Bible didn't go into detail about feeding and diaper changing - not that I want specifics on that part - TMI. Since Bubba didn't sin, how did he make his wishes known? Was an angel nudging you to the baby at feeding time? Was Buddy planning a thought in your head?"

Miss Mary "Gwen, you have to remember that even as a baby, he was still God." She explained how it worked but I can't reveal it here.

"Cool, so to both of you, some of my friends on earth, believed that Bubba did miracles as a child. Did he really do things like that?" One question led to a progression of two proud parents telling the story of their child's life story. I was glad Bubba was there to hear it. It's one thing to know something; it's another to hear it.

I told Mr. Joseph about a sermon my Dad preached and then repeated at HUMC about Joseph being Bubba's adopted father how that was special to me as an adopted child.

"What about those brothers mentioned in Acts 1:14 ? Some believe Joseph was a widow and brought these children into the marriage. What was the truth ? I didn't want to intimate details - just things seem to divide us on earth that really don't have bearing to the message. It seems important to some."

Bubba "Gwennie, I think that's enough for today. You can always talk to them again if you think of more questions."

"I really enjoyed your time today. Before you leave, we have a little something for you. "

I ran and picked up two gifts from the table.

One read: "To Mary From: Jesus"

The other read: "To Joseph From Jesus"

"Mom, this one is for standing me even to the cross and beyond." [John 19:25]

Miss Mary opened the gift. It was a locket with Bubba's baby picture on side and a small sliver of the cross on another. I could tell she liked it.

"Joseph, this one is for listening to the angels and being my adopted earthly father, as Gwennie puts it."

Mr. Joseph opened his which was a tiny angel.

The couple left. Bubba remained.

Bubba asked "Was it what you imagined?"

I had to think about that...I wondered if I'll learn more as my lunches progress.

"Bubba, do you have home movies from when you were a baby and a little boy?"

"Gwennie, no videos in Bethlehem."

"Bubba, it's Heaven. Surely, if you are in past, present, and future, there is a way to show a video clip."

"Do you want a movie night?"

"I think it would be fun."

"Not if you are the infant."

"I'm sure you were precious."

"Let's walk out to the porch."

As we sat on the Gwennie-size swing, a dark sky appear with a bright star. I couldn't believe it "Heavenly Home Movies". I love it. We watched as the baby turned into a toddler...the only thing I will say is there were no terrible two's.

THE THIRD LUNCH

I'm an early riser even in Heaven. I'm surprised that we can sleep given that it's light all the time. However, it works.

As I did on the first morning, I rise with a different devotion in mind. Today, I do quote scripture. I can't believe that I remember the psalms but I do. I wonder if it is something that happens when you cross through the gates. You enter his gates with Thanksgiving [Psalm 100:4] so maybe you are imprinted with the psalms to sing or say as you desire.

So Bubba has promised another guest for today. I'm excited! Mary and Joseph were enlightening yesterday - I can't wait to see what I learn today.

I take my time getting ready this morning. I have all the time in Heaven! Right!

I'm still on the hunt for that black bag. I still can't find it. Yesterday, I tried the downstairs. I start looking in the upstairs this morning. I start with my room. I look in the drawers and clothes. Up on shelves and under the bed. Nothing.

I decide to start from one end and work my way down. I'm working away looking until I notice the paintings on the wall. They are the same as the ones I purchased for my home - and then some that are really well-known pieces. I actually touch them to see if they are computer-generated or feel like canvas. They feel like canvas - so this is really good. I'm impressed. I get carried away so I have to hurry downstairs for my guests.

At the door, Bubba arrives with a man. I'm at a loss. There are several men that I wanted to meet while I'm up here. I don't recognize him from any Sunday School picture. I don't recognize him from any picture from recent history.

Bubba says "Quit trying to guess and I'll introduced you. Moses, please meet Gwen. Gwen, this is Moses."

We exchanged greetings.

"Bubba, he doesn't look like Charlton Heston."

I invited the gentlemen back to the sun porch.

After we sat and I introduced the menu - this time we were having something a little fancier since both were royalty - at least by southern standards. We had fried green tomatoes for starter, salad, baked salmon (with manna for a while and the fishes and loaves - I thought fish would be a good choice), and spinach maria.

"Moses, I'm so excited to meet you. I have heard your story since I was a child."

"Gwen, you have me at a disadvantage as I didn't grow up hearing Gwen stories when I was a child. Tell me a little about yourself."

Bubba laughed "This story was only in the Gwen James Version of the Bible."

I started "Like you Moses, I was adopted. It's one of the reasons your story appealed to me. However, it wasn't an open adoption like yours. I didn't know my birth family."

I did a little more telling.

"So Moses, I know that you had some time with your birth family before you were handed back to Pharaoh's daughter. [Exodus 2: 7-9] Did your birth family have enough time to teach you about the True God?"

Moses answered "How much do you remember from when you were 2, Gwen?"

"Okay, I'll give you that."

"However, Pharaoh's Daughter knew that you were Hebrew [Exodus 2: 6]. When did you learn that you were her adopted son?"

Moses shared how he learned of his adoption and his Hebrew roots. Let me just say it wasn't like the movie.

"I was adopted into a Christian family; one that was grounded in the Faith. When you learned the truth about your birth, how did you know the True God from the gods that the Egyptians worshiped like Ra ?"

Moses said "Well, there was the burning bush! [Exodus 3] Just kidding, Jesus told me that you like to laugh on the way to lunch. I'll tell you."

It's was interesting to learn how others that didn't have my Christian upbringing came to be a follower. It's inspiring the lengths that Buddy will go to find that lost sheep or what/who he will use.

"You know that line about 'you are to say to the Israelites : "I AM has sent me to you.' My Uncle Joe loved that he even made "I AM" his license plate." [Exodus 3:14]

"So you go to the new Pharaoh and demand that he free your people. Doesn't work. You do everything that Papa instructs you to do. Are you not fearful?"

Moses tells the story from his point of view with his thoughts and feelings. Very interesting - besides to think he was 80 [Exodus 7:7] when God was using him.

"You know the favorite part of the story is when Papa sets a trap for Pharaoh. I love the part where you say 'Do not be afraid. Stand firm and you will see the deliverance the Lord will bring you today. The Egyptians you see today you will never see again. The Lord will fight for you; you need only to be still.' I used that a few

times myself. 'The Lord will fight for me; I need only be still'."
[Exodus 14:13-14]

Bubba "Again, with the Gwen James Version of the Bible!"

"If it helped me remember the important stuff, then I think was okay. Moses it seems like every time you turned around those Israelites were grumbling about something. [Exodus 16:3, Exodus 17:2, Exodus 32:1] I often wondered how they could so quickly they could forget what it was like in Egypt."

Bubba "Moses wouldn't know their hearts. You and I can discuss that some time."

"Moses, it's been great meeting you today. Thanks for taking time to talk to me today. We have a little something for you."

I picked up the pink package from the front table and gave it to Bubba.

Bubba gave it to Moses saying "Thanks for leading our people out of Egypt. You inspired generations to follow."

Moses took the package. I'm not sure if he had ever seen a pink package wrapped with a perfect pick bow.

When he opened it, I explained "It's a toy. It's stiff now but shake it. "

He did.

"See it becomes like a snake! Buddy and I thought it was funny!"

I laughed. Not sure Moses enjoyed it but I think Buddy was laughing!

Moses departed.

Bubba remained.

"Gwennie, we have a few more lunches. Do you want to take a day off ? We have all the time in the "world"."

"Are you trying to make me laugh? No I want to keep going."

"Okay, I'll see you tomorrow. By the way, NO WORRYING in Heaven. I'll help you find the black bag when it's time."

"Yes, Rabbi. I stand corrected."

THE FOURTH LUNCH

On the next morning, I awoke to singing. Now this is what people thought Heaven would be like. Everyone singing. However, I don't think it was this type of singing. I had envisioned Handel's Messiah or other high brow stuff. These songs had some toe-tapping, hand-raising, maybe even praise-dancing potential.

I quickly jumped out of bed and readied myself.

I followed the sounds to the porch that I had shared with Papa and Bubba. Bubba was right my eyes had cleared some. I was starting to see others around the neighborhood. They were standing on their porches singing. I didn't see a worship pastor, praise team, or giant projection screen - no one had a hymnal for those wondering, but everyone was singing along.

I joined right in. It was a wonderful thing to enjoy corporate devotion time. We sang some songs that I remember from childhood full of reverence and awe. We sang those old gospel songs. We sang the new songs that we hear on Christian Radio. I declare my porch the "hand-raising" section of Heaven. Patty you are still welcome to visit!

I wonder how the songs are all familiar to me ! Not everyone could have been listening to the same stuff as me. I am going to ask Bubba about this at lunch because I think something is up!

As I have that thought, I hear laughter.

Bubba has let himself in with two more guests.

"Welcome. I apologize for not greeting you at the door."

The first guest says "No problem. It seems like you were caught but may I ask why Jesus laughed."

"Only silly Gwen tricks. I'm Gwen by the way."

"I'm Hadassah, but you may know me as Esther and this is my Uncle Mordecai." [Esther 2:7]

"Wow, Bubba, this is going to be good. Esther, I'm a sucker for a romance story. Yours is one of the best in the Bible! In addition, you kind of adopted by Mordecai like I was."

We gather in the sun room as was Bubba's and I tradition now. Today, we had chicken salad with grapes like Mom made. It was good. The guests seem to like it. Since we had a healthy lunch, we indulged with a sweet treat of banana pudding, like MawMaw Mary made.

We chatted a while before Bubba prompted me with my questions.

"How were you prepared for this happening? It had to come as a shock. I mean there was already a Queen."

Mordecai talked a little about their background and what they were doing. Bubba filled in some from THEIR perspective.

"Esther, how were the girls actually gathered for this contest?" [Esther 2:8]

Esther and Mordecai took turns explaining the times and how these things happened in those days. They reminded me that Mordecai knew where Esther was and walk outside the courtyard to what was happening to her. [Esther 2:11]

"Mordecai, how did you know that Esther should not reveal her true identity when she was part of the harem? Was there Anti-Semitism during that time?" [Esther 2:10]

Mordecai gave me the history on how they ended up in this situation. He told me about the land and their views.

"Esther, what was it like to have a year worth of spa treatments?" [Esther 2:12]

She just laughed.

"I think I could take if for a while but I'm not sure I could take it for that long! I would have to be doing something. It seemed to work for you because everyone loved you." [Esther 2:8-9, 15,17]

"Mordecai, I have never had a 'for such a time as this' moment but what a great line. I love it." [Esther 4:14]

Mordecai "Thanks, I think the part about you would not be spared was more impactful. What do you think Esther?" [Esther 4:13]

Esther just smiled.

"Esther, it doesn't mention anything about your faith or your heritage in the early part of my story. We talked a little bit about how you and Mordecai were prepared. Why was fasting something you thought of doing? Why your handmaids? Were they Hebrews, or had they adopted your beliefs? Why three days? Why two banquets? Did you know that Mordecai had been honored before you spoke at the second banquets?" [Esther 4:15-16, Esther 5:4, Esther 5:7]

Esther tried to answer my questions as I rapidly fired them off - of course, I had been through several studies of this book and read it so many times. I had seen the movie. I had even watched the Veggie Tales video several times (yes, I'm too old for it, so do not judge!) and loved Mordecai, Pa Grape! I had these waiting for a while.

"I promise this is the last one. Did you live happily ever after?"

Mordecai and Esther just looked at me, but Bubba laughed (I heard Buddy laughing in my head!)

When Mordecai and Esther left, I asked Bubba to stay.

"Bubba, why was this book in the Bible? I understand that it gave the history of Purim, but it doesn't even mention God?"

"Gwennie, it wasn't meant to be revealed all it once. We have a while."

THE FIFTH LUNCH

I stretched as I awoke. It's great waking without an alarm like a permanent weekend. I sleep so well here. I don't need the TV to lull me to sleep. My mind doesn't go back over the day thinking of things I could have done better. It doesn't race ahead to tomorrow worrying about what might happen. It's very liberating. I wish I had more of that peace before THE DOOR. It probably would have made my time there more enjoyable for me and others around me. Too late now and here there are no regrets - just realizations and truths about my journey.

Okay, I am so into my deep thinking that I just realize no singing this morning. I wonder if there is a guide somewhere that tell which days are singing days and which are not. Maybe a Heavenly Headliner which a calendar of events! I might be helpful! I don't want to miss anything! Need to ask about that next time I see Bubba!

I decided that today I'd take an iced tea. No, I never liked coffee, so I went out on the porch and did my devotion there. Today, as I watch the monitor that Papa and I watched the first night, I see something totally new and unexpected.

It was broadcasting a live feed from the Throne room. I only recognized it from John's writing. [Revelation 4]. I didn't recognize Papa seated in the Throne. It was something so overwhelming.

"Holy, holy, holy, Lord God Almighty! Early in the Morning, our song shall rise to thee; holy, holy, merciful and mighty! God in three Persons blessed Trinity!

Holy, holy, holy, all the saints adore thee, Casting down their golden crowns around the glassy sea; Cherubin and seraphim falling down before thee, Who wert, and art, and evermore shalt be.

Holy, holy, holy, Lord God Almighty! All they works shall praise they name, in earth, and sky, and sea; Holy, holy, holy; merciful and mighty! God in three Persons blessed Trinity!"

Sometimes Number 1 in the Old Baptist Hymnal will only do.

Standing at his right side (I can say that with certainty because in Heaven I finally know my left from my right!), Bubba is talking. I think this is the pleading part on our behalf. [Acts 2:33,1 John 2:1]

"Before the throne of God above

I have a strong and perfect plea:

A great high priest, whose name is Love,

Whoever lives and pleads for me.

My name is graven on his hands,

My name is written on his heart;

I know that while in heaven He stands,

no tongue can bid me thence depart

no tongue can bid me thence depart.

When Satan tempted me to despair,

And told me of the guilt within

Upward I looked, and saw him there

Who made an end to all my sin.

Because a sinless Savior died,

my sinful soul is counted free;

For God, the Just, is satisfied,

To look on Him and pardon me

To Look on Him and pardon me.

Hallelujah!

Hallelujah!

Praise the One,

Risen Son of God!

Hallelujah!

Hallelujah!

Praise the One,

Risen Son of God!

Hallelujah!

Hallelujah!

Praise the One,

Risen Son of God!

Then a little Shane & Shane or Selah depending on your preference but the words were actually written in the 1800's by Charitie Lees Bancroft. Vikki Cook wrote the tune in 1997.

I look around people are starting to come out on their porches. I can tell some are doing as I did and having quiet meditation, and others are having hand-raising, toe-tapping, and praise-dancing times. I can't hear any of it. Heaven is a curious place.   I have a while to figure this out, and I like puzzles.

I take my time this morning just enjoying the view.

Bubba calls from the formal parlor "Gwennie, your guests have arrived."

"I'm coming."

When I greet the guests, the woman reminds me of someone but I can't tell who.

The little girl speaks up "Hi, I'm Susan. Bubba said that you knew me. So do you?"

"I said that Gwen knew about you. She is going to get to know you."

I couldn't believe it. It was Susan, my sister, who I never met in my life. In fact, she passed before I was even born.

"Susan, it's a pleasure to meet you. I'm Gwen, your sister."

Susan looked bewildered. I'm not sure if she understood her sister or if everyone is a sister here, so it wasn't much of a statement.

The other woman grabbed me in a hug. I was a little taken aback because most greetings had been handshakes or bows to this point - at least with strangers. She stretched out her arms to take a good look at me. I still thought I might know her and since she hugged me, I think I knew her well.

Bubba "I'll cut in here. Gwen, this is your Grandmother Weinberg."

"Hi MawMaw! You are a looker! I don't remember you looking this good in our pictures from your youth."

"We have our own version of plastic surgery up here!"

"Since I kept you waiting, let's go into the sun room."

Bubba "We didn't mind waiting. I enjoyed today's devotion. We can discuss your questions after lunch."

I think this is going to be a little different lunch. I don't need any questions. I think I'll be answering them today.

As we sit down, I realize the meal that is before us. It's a holiday meal that MawMaw would have fixed. Because it is heaven, we have two kinds of giblet gravy, one with giblets and one without! You can guess the kind I will be having.

"Susan, have you had one of these holiday dinners before?" I ask.

"What's a holiday dinner?"

"It's a time with a family, everyone you love, gets together to eat."

"So like today?"

"Yes, just like today."

"Susan, this is just like the ones that MawMaw cooked for us years ago - but the best part is she didn't have to slave away in the kitchen and we don't have to do the dishes."

I just got a blank stare. I guess the window to earth to see happy things doesn't exist. I think, "Bubba, has someone been remiss in her training?" - "Gwennie, wait for it."

"Susan, let's start you will turkey and mashed potatoes. I am thinking you want gravy sans giblets."

"I don't know what that means but okay."

MawMaw and I reminisce about times. Since I don't think that window to Earth is working, I tell her about the good stuff that has happened since she came to Heaven.

Bubba says "Dartha, I think you had a question or two."

"Gwen, why did you call me that Sunday afternoon?"

"MawMaw, it's a long story about that Easter weekend . Bubba might have to remind me about some points. It started on a Good Friday which I had off from work. I decided to bless people as I drove from Nashville to Knoxville to visit Mom and Dad. I started at Mrs. Winner's for an iced tea, started my blessings there, and continued one with one stop and another. I never told anyone about these stops, and the details aren't important, at least in the story.

On Friday night, Mom, Dad, and I attended a play at Faith Promise Church in Knoxville. It was about the passion of Christ but it displayed all the forces of light and darkness fighting this battle. It was so powerful. I couldn't keep from weeping.

I couldn't sleep much that night - I ended up watching a video of <u>Facing the Giants,</u> you might remember Sherwood Baptist Church where we were in Albany - Sherwood Pictures did this movie. I must have watched that movie at least 3 times that weekend.

I can't remember what I did Saturday.

Bubba interjected.

"On Sunday, we went to church and it was moving. I left that weekend on the way home feeling like I had an encounter with God. Praying and Praising THEM in the car on the way home. I cut of the radio and just listened. I just knew that Buddy was guiding me to do 3 things before I went to bed that night.

1. I had to rid my house of the romance novels that I loved so much.

2. I had to write something that Buddy had impressed on me.

3. I had to call you.

I don't remember much more of the right. I just became more and more convinced it wasn't me but Buddy.

The first two were easy. I ended up with 6 black trash bags of novels. The story just leaped onto the page. Then I was left with the call.

I had to take a break.

I had to pray again - it would not be easy.

I got comfortable, picked up the phone, and dialed. You answered. I explained the reason for my call. I thought it was a good talk. Don't you?"

"Yes, and I have never told anyone about what we discussed!"

"I know ! Sherry Marie told Mom you mentioned it to her but that you couldn't tell Sherry what we discussed that night. It was after you had the stroke on that Friday night. I'll never get over the fact that on Sunday I called because I knew I had to and on Friday the chance to hear the story would have been gone even though you lived for a few more years."

Bubba got up and retrieved two packages from the table in the hall.

"For you Dartha, from Gwennie and Me. It's for shining the light of truth into her life. It meant that she didn't have to carry that darkness anymore."

MawMaw opened the package as Bubba said "Gwen and Buddy were responsible for picking this presents."

MawMaw stared down at the spoon in the package which a confused look. I told her to find PawPaw and ask him how to use it to stir a pot!

The second package was for Susan, who had just read this story. I'm sure she was bored so I said "Next time you visit, we will do something fun."

Bubba said "Susan, thanks to you. Gwennie got a family that loved the Lord so one of my little lambs came home."

Susan did what she had seen MawMaw do with her package and with a little more excitement. Inside was a puffy dress like the one I wore on Easter, complete with black patent shoes.

"Maw Maw made sure I looked good on Easter so we thought you might like to have a dress like this."

We said our goodbyes for now. MawMaw and I promised to meet again because we never got the opportunity to exchange stories like we discussed that Sunday night.

The guests left.

Bubba and I went out to the porch. We talked about the peace I found because of that night and that I knew that it was one of the times I knew Buddy and He were working. I need that light or it would have haunted me.

"Bubba, I've enjoyed these lunches but I feel like I need a job."

"We have something in mind."

"Does it have something to do with the Game?"

"You can guess and try to figure out this puzzle but for now let's watch the monitor."

I turn and see the monitor rolling...I start to laugh.

It's Veggie Tales and Mordecai the Pea!

Just what I needed!

MUSIC CLASS

The night before I had mentioned to Bubba that I thought it was time to take a break from the Luncheons and move onto my job. I wake up thinking about that job assignment.

I begin my morning by stopping off to grab an Iced Tea before heading out on the porch. Because I'm thinking of that new job. A song comes to mind...

> Here am I, send me, Lord;
>
> Here am I, send me, Lord;
>
> Make my life useful to Thee.
>
> Here am I, send me, Lord;
>
> Here am I, send me, Lord;
>
> Make my life useful to Thee.

[Take my life, lead me, Lord.   R. Maines Rawls (1968). LANGLEY. United Methodist Hymnal]

After devotions, I had back upstairs to get ready for my first day at work. I hope they have a power suit in the closet. When I return the bedroom, I find a summer blowy dress. Not what I would pick for the first day of a new job. Obviously, SOMEONE thinks differently than I - let's just guess!

I'm back down stairs when the doorbell rings.

Outside I find Bubba and Susan, I'm a little surprised to see Susan for a day at the office. I'm sure that's where we are heading. After all, I did train on Earth in Corporate America!

Bubba heads off my train of thought by saying out loud "I know you said last night that you wanted a job but Papa and I thought you still need a little time to get orientated to Heaven. Susan wanted to show you things she does so We thought this would be just the ticket!"

"I can't argue with the perfect one so Susan where are we headed?"

Susan says "Music class! Follow Me!"

Bubba "I'll leave you girls to it. I need to greet someone at the Gates."

"Another Slider?"

"No Gwennie, Buddy is carrying this one. No tears! Only Joy at a Homecoming!"

Susan and I head in the opposite direction. We pass houses and houses. I wonder who leaves in them. Susan can name some but not all. I guess we will learn them as we go along here.

We reach a grassey, green field. Other little children are already gathered around a man sitting on a road.

Susan "It looks like Teacher is ready to start."

"Okay, but let's sit in the back because I'm taller than the little ones."

The teacher says let's begin with our favorite shall we...

All the children begin signing in the sweetest choir ever. I just wish they had on the cute little short white robes and were sitting on the steps at the front of the Church. I then realize the song has different words than I remember!

> Jesus Loves me! this I know, For He tells me so;
>
> Little ones belong to him; they are weak, but he is strong.
>
> Yes, Jesus love me, Yes, Jesus love me,
>
> Yes, Jesus loves me, For He tells me so.
>
> [Jesus Loves Me, Anna B. Warner, Tune China, William B. Bradbury, Baptist Hymnal]

The teacher says, "Stand up and try it with the hand motion." We stand and the little ones start signing the song. I know the "Yes, Jesus love me " part so I join in then.

> The leader starts the chorus...
>
> "And I shall dwell in the house of the Lord forever,
>
> And I shall feast at the table spread for me
>
> Surely goodness and mercy shall follow me

All the days, all the days of my life, All the days, all the days of my life.

[Surely Goodness and Mercy. John W. Peterson and Alfred B. Smith Copyright 1958, Baptist Hymnal]

We sign this course a few times. We go on to sign more that I don't recognize.

Finally the teacher says "Time is almost up. Do you want to hear one that I wrote?"

The kids are all for it!

He takes an instrument I am not familiar with and begins playing.

"I will extol the Lord at all times'

his praise will always be on my lips.

My soul will boast in the Lord;

let the afflicted hear and rejoice.

Glorify the LORD with me;

Let us exalt his name together.

I sought the LORD, and he answered me;

he delivered me from all my fears.

Those who look to him are radiant;

their faces are never covered with shame.

This poor man called, and the LORD heard him;

He saved him out of all his troubles.

The angel of the LORD encamps around those who fear him,

and he delivers them.

Come, my children, listen to me;

I will teach you the fear of the LORD.

Whoever of you love life

and desires to see many good days,

keep your tongue from evil

and your lips from speaking lies,

Turn from evil and do good;

seek peace and pursue it.

The eyes of the Lord are on the righteous

and his ears are attentive to their cry;

the face of the LORD is against those who do evil,

to cut off the memory of them from the earth.

A righteous man may have many troubles,

but the LORD delivers him from them all;

He protects all his bones,

not one of them will be broken.

Evil will slay the wicked;

the foes of the righteous will be condemned.

The LORD redeems his servants;

no one will be condemned who taxes refuge

in him.

[Psalms 34 NIV]

Half way into the song, I figure out the "teacher". This experience will teach me to be early for such events! I hear Laughter in my head!

"Class Dismissed"

The Kids run off in all directions. I not sure where they are going.

Susan takes my hand "You have to meet the Teacher! Teacher, this is my sister, Gwennie. She just arrived."

"You can call me 'Gwen'."

He says "I heard you would be joining us. Jesus tells me that you had a few specific of my songs you liked."

I am not sure he knows chapters, so I have just the first lines of a couple I have used in the past...

"I used 'The LORD is my shepherd; I shall not want.' [Psalm 23] and 'Have Mercy on me, O God, according to your unfailing love; according to your great compassion blot out my transgressions. [Psalm 51]

David replies "I'm glad they were useful. Maybe we will see you in class some other time. Bye Susan. Nice meeting you Gwennie."

As we walk away, I ask Susan, please arrive a little earlier for the next event. I want to meet the leaders before the sessions.

More laughter!

ARTS AND CRAFTS

Susan and I head to the next event. I'm relieve to find it in a large room with spacious counter space. I see a man at the front.

I ask Susan to introduce us.

Susan very politely says "Teacher, this is my big sister who likes to be called Gwen. Gwen, this is teacher."

The teacher says, "I would like to be called Reuben."

"Hi, Reuben, it's nice to meet you. I hope that it's okay that I'm joining Susan today."

Reuben replied "THEY told me you were coming so I set up a station for you next to Susan. I think you are going to enjoy this class."

When Susan leads me to the table, I see long strips of different colored cloth and different materials to attach them. I am already thinking Joseph's coat of many colors. However, I would have thought Joseph would be teaching. I'm not sure who Reuben is in this story. I should have paid attention in Sunday School.

Reuben says "Let's begin today by working on the project. You are to construct a coat for yourself out of the strips of cloth on your table. You can use anything on your table or around the room you like. Remember what we say here: Arts and Crafts?"

The kids sound "ALL ART IS BEAUTIFUL EVEN PURPLE COWS!" and they all laugh!

We start working on our project. I'm getting into it. I'm much better at sewing than I thought. In no time, we all have beautiful coats that exactly fit us. They all look different but everyone looks happy!

Reuben gathers us around a floor mat to the back of the room.

Reuben begins "Let me tell you about these coats and why we made them today. A long time ago, a daddy had a special coat made for his son, Joseph. Joseph was his favorite son - even though his father had many sons. This coat was just another thing that made the brothers mad.

A plan was made to kill Joseph. However, something stopped the brothers. The first threw him in a pit. When an Egyptian trader happened by, they decided to make a little money off of him so they sold Joseph to the trader.

Joseph endure many things when he was in Egypt. Not good things but we now from other story that the FATHER makes good things happen out of bad things. That's where the story gets good.

The King of Egypt, they called him Pharaoh, heard about how Joseph knew what dreams meant. The King had been having weird dreams and no one else could figure them out. The King finally called for Joseph. Joseph knew what the dream meant because GOD had told him.

Joseph told the King, "Egypt would have 7 years of great harvest and more than enough food. Then it would have 7 years with not much food. You should store food during the good years to have food for the bad ones. Place someone wise over the project." The King was so impressed that he made Joseph second in command in Egypt only under the King.

So it happened as Joseph had promised because GOD told me so.

It so happened that the rest of Joseph's family also experienced the bad years. They came to Egypt to obtain food. Joseph does test his brothers a little but he in the end let's his brothers know he is the brother wanted to kill.

The other brothers were really scared.

Joseph said "Don't be afraid. Because you didn't send me here, GOD did. He made a way to help our family during the time without food. "

Joseph forgave his brothers.

Do you know why you made the coats that made the brothers mad?"

Little hands flew up.

Reuben said "Susan, do you have an answer?"

My smart little sister said "Joseph's daddy had only one favorite. GOD is our daddy and we are all his favorites."

Reuben answered her "You have been paying attention. Good job Susan. That's it for today. Let's clean up, and you will be dismissed."

They knew the "Clean up, Clean up" song so they work went well.

After I clean my work station, I walked up to Reuben to asked how he fit into the story. Before I could ask, he said "I was told to tell you Genesis 37:21-22. Jesus said to look for the Gideon's Bible in the drawer next to your bed."

"How do you know what I was going to ask? Are you able to read minds?"

Reuben said "No, I only repeat what GOD or Jesus tell me."

"Thank you for an interesting talk. I can't wait to read the verses to find out the rest of the story. It was a pleasure meeting you."

Reuben invited me back any time.

Susan and I soon departed.

THE WORLD MAP

I'm hungry all this music and crafts make a girl hungry. I asked Susan if she was hungry and if we had time to find something to eat before our next appointment. She knows just the spot.

We find the spot. A Burger joint. Perfect! I've been healthy even in heaven. I need a juicy burger with cheese. We enjoyed our lunch and talked about the last stop. It's with Paul. I think it's the one of Saul/Paul fame [Acts 9:1-18]. Susan says he tells adventure stories. I wonder if he talks about violence in some of his stories. Some aren't very pretty [Acts 14:19 for example].

We hurry to the next last stop of the day.

The session was filling up. Paul stood in front of a room with theater seating and a big screen behind him. The stadium seats were filled with about 1/2 children and 1/2 adults. Apparently, this was a popular session.

Paul called the session to order.

He began with a praise song. I had never heard but several people sang along. I wondered to myself if it was the same one that loosed those chains. [Acts 16:23-31] I wonder if we will have a question and answer session.

He started by explaining that people in today's world know the world is round and have documented almost every known part.

Some of the deep parts are still unknown to man. He showed a map of the world as it is known in today's world.

Paul states "In my day, I want you to see the world map as we drew it." He pointed out Jerusalem and Rome. He showed us how far man had travelled by water (barring the Great Flood). Then he went through his travels, mentioning how GOD had directed him to certain places. He talked about the people that he met along the way.

Paul then said "Watch this!"

The map light up with a tiny pin point light. It followed the route he described in his travels. Sometimes it was white; sometimes it was yellow. He explained during those yellow times his faith was being tested by others. He had to stand for Jesus even in prison and hardships. [Acts 20:23] The light would turn white again as he would be lead to move on in his travels. It moves through the arrest and trip to Rome [Acts 27]. It finally turns out.

Paul says "I finished the race and completed the task the Lord Jesus had given me. [Acts 20:24, According to Church Tradition Paul was beheaded during the time of Nero] Now, let's watch the route again."

This time each time Paul's light traveled to a place other lights would join his. As his left, little clusters would grow.

Paul further explained "They would have called me a Missionary today. I called myself "An Apostle - sent not from men nor by man, but by Jesus Christ and God the Father, who raised him from the dead". [Galatians 1:1]. There were other men who were travelling and preaching as well. Look at the map now."

The map add lights in other areas.

Paul "I'm going to do a slow progression without narration to let you look at how the world map changes as Man explores but also how the lights move."

This progression is amazing to watch as the map expands and more pin lights are added. Then I notice that some areas are darking as pin lights fade.

Paul interjects "The original pin lights have died and the people are not following The Way in those areas. See here as he points to one area."

He then continues the progression. He is silent as we make our way to current day.

Paul leaves the map up but moves to the side.

He asks "Now would anyone like to know any more about we have seen?"

The hands shoot up but mine remains in my lap.

I'm memorized by the map. The children might not have learned borders in school but I have a general idea of where countries are. Now, I'm wishing I had paid more attention. I am taking a good guess about some areas. I'm surprised by what I see.

I had heard about strong underground churches in repressive regimes. The pin lights confirmed those stories. I'll have to ask Bubba how Buddy is managing to get the WORD there.

The other part is breaking my heart. Other places I expected pin lights are dark. I wonder is there still time for them or is the game almost over.

Bubba says in my head "No weeping in heaven [opposite of Matthew 8:12]. There is always hope. [1 Cor. 13 : 7]

I reply in my head "What's the score?"

Bubba "Still 1-0 with the Whites in the lead."

Soon the class is over. Susan and I walk out of the class room without speaking to Paul. I add him to my list of people that I want to have over for lunch sometime.

"Are there anymore sessions today?"

Thankfully, Susan says "No, it's fun time now! Do you want an ice cream?"

I'm up for that! I've been denying myself because of my weight on earth, so I will enjoy this one.

"What kinds to they have?"

"Any kind you can imagine?"

I thought "Of course, how silly of me."

We head for the ice cream. When we reach there, Susan selects Vanilla. I'm like "what?" I select Pistachio!

With cones in hand, we turn toward my house.

I ask "Susan, do you know if I'm supposed to go somewhere with you tomorrow?" It's too late. I remember the rule, 'Participate, don't Anticipate!

"Bubba, usually lets me know what I will be doing in the morning."

We say good-bye at my door.

It's been a great day!

THE FIELD TRIP

The next morning, I decide to do devotions like I did at home. I put on my walking gear. Since it's nice out, I start walking around the street. I start with Praise...

There's a line that's been drawn through the ages;

On that line stands the old rugged cross.

On that cross a battle is raging

For the gain of a man's soul or its loss.

On one side march the forces of evil,

All the demons and devils of hell;

On the other the angels of glory,

And they meet on Golgotha's hill.

The earth shakes with the force of the conflict;

The sun refuses to shine,

For there hangs God's Son in the balance,

And then through the darkness He cries—

It is finished! The battle is over.

It is finished! There'll be no more war.

It is finished! The end of the conflict.

It is finished! And Jesus is Lord!

Yet in my heart the battle was raging;

Not all pris'ners of war had come home.

These were battlefields of my own making;

I didn't know that the war had been won.

Then I heard that the King of the Ages

Had fought all my battles for me,

And vict'ry was mine for the claiming,

And now, praise His name I was free!

It is finished! The battle is over.

It is finished! There'll be no more war.

It is finished! The end of the conflict.

It is finished! And Jesus is Lord!

[It is Finished. Bill and Gloria Gaither]

Then it's just inside my head talking to Papa, Bubba, and Buddy as I have always done. I find myself looking for my phone app to see how many steps or minutes I have done.

It feels about right so I turn in the opposite direction and head home.

I get ready for the day; again, someone has left an outfit on my bed complete with hard hat. It has "Gwennie" printed on it. No steeled toe shoes or safety glasses.

I hurry down stairs excited about today's adventure.

Bubba and Susan (who is decked out as I am with her own personalized hard hat) are waiting in the parlor.

"Sorry to keep you waiting."

Bubba "That's okay. You are worth it."

"So where are we headed?"

Susan " He isn't telling! It's a surprise! Do you like our matching hats?"

"I do. We will have to get more matching hats!"

Bubba escorts us out of the house and in the direction of our field trip. We are going in a direction I have never been headed. Eventually, we come to a big building. It's not like any of the houses.

Bubba says "It's the tear warehouse tour you wanted." [Psalms 56:8]

"Oh boy, Susan - this is going to be great. I wish I had a paper and pen so I flowchart it."

Susan "What is flowcharting?"

Bubba "Susan, never mind. I'm leaving you here. Ask for Fred. I'll be back to pick you up when you are finished. Enjoy the tour."

Susan and I enter the building. We tell the receptionist that Fred expecting us. She calls him and relays that he is on his way.

He comes to the back door in a hurry.

Fred "I understand you are here for a tour."

"Yes, I wanted to see this since I've been here."

Fred "Well, follow me and we will begin. You know you don't need the hard hats. Nothing ever falls here. No OSHA accidents ever."

"Well, we like to match so we will keep on our hats" said Susan

We walk through the door. There are rows and rows of shelving stacked to the ceiling, but the first thing I noticed was that there was no sound. I don't hear any other people speaking. No beeping from backing forklifts or any machinery at all. Interesting.

Fred asked "Where do you want to begin?"

Gwen "I also like to start with the beginning. Where to the tears come in?"

We walk back to the warehouse. Again, I'm not seeing anyone else.

"Fred, how many shifts do you run at the warehouse?"

Fred "The Warehouse is always open."

"Fred, how many people work in the warehouse?"

"Two, myself and receptionist."

I'm on high alert now. Segregation of Duties issues flag.

I guess this is Heaven so I don't need to check if the doors are locked.

We reach the in-take table.

Fred "It all starts here. The tears come in and I place them in the appropriate jar."

I ask "How do you retrieve the appropriate jar? Is the Warehouse equipped with RF scanners and bin location system so you know where a jar is located?"

Fred" No, it is right here when it's needed." He pulls one from the rack and falls a tear. He places the jar exactly where he retrieved it.

We watch for a few moments as additional tears fall into different jars which he keeps pulling from the same place.

I ask "Are they the same jar?"

Fred "No. See you can tell by the shape."

Me "Do they have names on them?"

Fred "Not that I can read."

Me "Let's test something. Can you retrieve my bottle?"

Fred takes the next jar off the same rack. I can read my name! I'm beginning to have an idea about my job in Heaven but I'll wait on Papa and Bubba to reveal it.

I thank Fred for the Tour.

I pull Susan along to the front. As I suspected, Bubba is waiting on us as we leave.

We walk back to the mansion and say good night.

I thank Bubba for our tour.

Then I found paper so I could draw a flowchart of the warehouse!
It's the weirdest one I've ever drawn!

ORIENTATION AND PREPARATION

As I wake the next morning, I go to the porch. The big screen has a picture of the throne room with Papa in his grandeur and Bubba to the side. Angels surround them singing to the Father. As I watch words appear on the screen, I sing along. It's in tune with the angels. I have joined the heavenly chorus! Wow! I always wondered at what they sang from their creation. I wonder if they sing the same song. I wonder if Papa likes different songs at different times. Did he have a different song when Bubba was on the cross? Maybe on that celebration I will learn!

After devotions, my screen is filled with Bubba as he is dressed normally - not as the King he is. He welcomed me to Employee Orientation and introduced me to Olive, who would guide me through this process.

Bubba "Buddy, thought you might know by now, what your job will be?"

Gwennie "I have a thought which you can read. See if I am correct."

Bubba "Already knew you were! My little sister has always been clever. Just not as clever as WE! I'll leave it to you, Olive."

Olive "Welcome to Orientation. I hope that you are adjusting to the rest of your life. It's interesting that you wanted your heaven to include a job other than praising the True God."

Gwennie "I guess is that little bit of Methodist in me...with my prayers, presence, gifts, and service. I guess that for entity. I need to praise him with all that He has given me."

Olive "As orientation, The Father and Jesus suggested we start with this video."

As the video rolled, I realized I was correct. I was some of my fondest memories from my time as a 1st grade teacher at Hermitage. I saw me reading the lessons and analyzing the verses in my multiple versions Bible looking for just the right version for the kids. I was writing the verses on the "teachers lined strips to put on the bulletin board".

I saw the time we had a slight "error" with the story of Jesus as a boy. The next time we had a story about the Jesus miracles, I asked a visually impaired couple to come. They showed how they read the Bible in Braille.

Then, we talked about missionaries, so I asked someone to come and talk about their recent mission trip to India. The couple decorated the room with items from India. They helped the girls dress in sari! It was great. I think the couple had as much fun as the kids.

I saw a few more times that I had forgotten about but that were just as much fun and still as dear. I don't know if they meant much to the kids but they did to me.

After the video, Olive said "The Father thought there are so many children here that never had a chance to go to Sunday School. They thought you might want that challenge to have a truly Heavenly Class!"

Gwennie "Would it be like on earth but better?"

Olive "Oh Yes"

Gwennie "Do I have a curriculum to follow?"

Olive "You know the curriculum. No publishing house needed here."

"Cool, I think I know where I'll start. Thanks Olive. What else do I need to know before I start?"

Olive "You will start tomorrow. Let me show you the classroom. "

The screen dissolved to show a classroom with little chairs and tables...and a large craft room to the side.

Olive "You should find anything for Arts & Crafts in that room. I'll pick you up tomorrow to show you the way to your class."

"Olive, thank you for your help."

I knew just where I would start. Now, to figure out what to do.

FIRST DAY ON THE JOB

The first day on the job I woke really early. I always had when I was working. I decided that I needed to do my walking and praying as I did on earth.

Just as I was, without one plea

But that Thy blood was shed for me

And that Thou bidst me came to Thee

O Lamb of God, I came, I came

Just as I was, and waiting no

To rid my soul of one dark blot

To Thee whose blood can cleanse each spot

O Lamb of God, I came, I came

I came broken to be mended

I came wounded to be healed

I came desperate to be rescued

I came empty to be filled

I came guilty to be pardoned

By the blood of Christ the Lamb

And I'm welcamed with open arms

Praise God, just as I was

Just as I was, I would be lost

But mercy and grace my freedom bought

And now to glory in Your cross

Oh Lamb of God, I came, I came

I came broken to be mended

I came wounded to be healed

I came desperate to be rescued

I came empty to be filled

I came guilty to be pardoned

By the blood of Christ the Lamb

And I was welcomed with open arms

Praise God, just as I was

I came broken to be mended

I came wounded to be healed

I came desperate to be rescued

I came empty to be filled

I came guilty to be pardoned

By the blood of Christ the Lamb

And I was welcomed with open arms

Praise God, just as I was

["Just as I am" by Travis Cottrell; original text by Charlotte Elliot in 1835]

After the walk, I dress for a fun class not what I would have for a Sunday morning class.

Olive arrives right on time so I can be earlier than the children. I have a bag with me that contains the snacks. Every good Sunday School has snacks. I want to inspect the classroom and gather my supplies.

We take a short walk and Olive drops me off at the classroom. I am able to explore on my own. I love it. Cabinets just for Sunday School! I love that! The room will be dedicated to Sunday School, so I can arrange it and do not have to set it back for Pre-K the next day! Lovely! This place is Heaven!

Okay, I have to get ready.

I found my teacher ruled strips of paper and copied the Bible verse for today.   Then I find just what I want for the craft.

Someone walks into the classroom.

"Hello, I understand that you requested that I tell you about the time I heard Jesus speak."

"Yes, I am so excited to have you. Today is my first class so I haven't meet the children but I think this is how the class will go. We will do brief introductions. Then tell your story. Do our Bible Verse. I scheduled another little visitor, if it can be arranged. Then we will do our arts and crafts. We will finish with Snack."

I could tell from the look on his face. I had lost him.

"I will point to you when you should tell your story. I think you will enjoy if you stay for the rest but if you want to leave, you may."

"Thank you."

I finish arranging the room as he just stares at me. I think this is a very new concept for him. Gwennie in action. I hope that Bubba and Papa are enjoying his reaction as much as I am.

The children arrive. I greet each one. I realize I don't have to make a game out of their names, which I remember easily. Again, I'm liking this heavenly version!

We gather in the story telling area.

"Welcome to Sunday School. We are going to have fun today. We are going to learn about what Jesus did on earth. We will do some fun crafts. We will also need some helpers."

In heaven no struggling to make everyone happy! They will all have a turn, so we start with the three who have raised their hands. I am sure that next time - another set will want to be the helpers.

"Before we start, we have two guests today. You see one here his name is Jonathan. Say "Hello". Another will be along shortly. Today we are going to learn about a story that Jesus told while on earth from someone who actually heard it!"

Jonathan explains "I was not really someone who many friends while I was living on earth but Jesus was my friend. He spent time with me and people like me. We went to hear him and he told us these stories. Jesus told one about this shepherd. The shepherd had 100 sheep but lost one. The shepherd leaves the other 99 in the open country and searches for that one that is lost. The shepherd is overjoyed when he finds the sheep. When the shepherd reaches home with now all 100, he calls all his friends and neighbors together so they can be excited with him."

The man goes on to tell the children that Jesus told a few more stories that day. [Luke 15]

One child finally asks "What is a sheep?"

I say "What a good question?"

In walks The Shepherd complete with a SHEEP! [Psalms 36:6 - besides God can do whatever he wants!] The children gather around The Shepherd and the little sheep. They pet the sheep and The Shepherd explains the meaning of the story Jonathan told them. [1 Corinthians 13:12] .

The Shepherd "I think that the sheep and I have a date with his lunch. Goodbye for now. Enjoy the rest of Sunday School."

I turn the children back to the class (and Jonathan stays).

"That story has a great Bible verse that we should hear...

> *Luke 15:7a : I tell you that in that same way there will be more rejoicing in heaven over the wicked person who changes his mind*

Can you say it with me?"

The children repeat it.

"Can you say it louder?"

This time, Jonathan joins in and it's loud.

"Let's see if we can make God hear it in the Throne room." We do still louder yet.

Bubba's voice is heard by all "We heard you...now listen. You should hear that rejoicing NOW!"

And we did! It was awesome. I hadn't heard that before - I wonder if you have be tuned to it. I'll have to ask that next time I see Bubba.

This week's Bible verse helper sticks the Bible verse on the bulletin board.

"Well now, I thought we would make our own sheep to take with us to remind us that Father is always looking for that lost sheep on earth. Let's move to the table. Each place as a sheep mold and your wool.   Each of you has your own glue. Start gluing and sticking. Remember it's all art!" I demonstrate on my own sheep. The joy of teaching is being able to do the arts and crafts as well!

I noticed that Jonathan also picked up his model and glued his wool.

As they finish their art work, I have them put it in their cubbies by the door and invite them back to the table.

No wool is falling off the little lamb models. I ask Jonathan to check my back to see if I am carrying wool back there. He says no. I learned that lesson on earth.

This week's snack helpers pass out the cups and napkins.

Jonathan helps pour the red punch. I figure this is heaven - no worries about spills! I pass out the graham crackers shaped like little sheep! I love teaching in Heaven. This is going to be so cool!

As the children finish their snack, they hug us and I tell them I can't wait until next time because it is so true.

Jonathan lingers.

"May I came back?" he asks.

"Of course, we would love to hear more of the stories that Jesus taught."

"I meant just to be here."

"Yes, you can be a co-teacher."

We say our good-byes.

I guess tax-collectors need 1st grade Sunday School as well.

SECOND DAY ON THE JOB

I awake thinking about the previous day. It was the even better than the goodness provided on earth. [Psalms 27:13] It was my favorite thing but so much better. As the ideas come into mind for classes, I know that They are leading me to redo classes I've taught on earth. I can't wait to see how this lesson is corrected from the way it went on earth. It's time to get out of this comfy bed and on with the day.

I grab that sweet tea on my way out the door for a walk this morning.

> I tried to fit you in the walls inside my mind
>
> I tried to keep you safely in between the lines
>
> I tried to put you in the box that I've designed
>
> I tried to pull you down so we are eye to eye
>
>
> When did I forget that you've always been the king of the world?
>
> I tried to take life back right out of the hands of the king of the world
>
> How could I make you so small
>
> When you're the one who holds it all

When did I forget that you've always been the king of the world

Just a whisper of your voice can tame the seas

So who was I to try to take the lead

Still I ran ahead and thought I was strong enough

When you're the one who made me from the dust

When did I forget that you've always been the king of the world?

I tried to take life back right out of the hands of the king of the world

How could I make you so small

When you're the one who holds it all

When did I forget that you've always been the king of the world

Ohhhh, you set it all in motion

Every single moment

You brought it all to me

And you're holding on to me

When did I forget that you've always been the king of the world?

I tried to take life back right out of the hands of the king of the world

How could I make you so small

When you're the one who holds it all

When did I forget you've always been the king of the world

You will always be the king of the world

[Natalie Grant]

I return to the mansion and ready myself for another fun-filled day. I think I'm ready for class. I check to see if I have everything I need; Then I head to the classroom.

Jonathan is already there!

"What are we doing today?"

I say, "We are going back a little to Jesus' life today."

We gather the supplies we need from the closet and discuss today's lesson. I copy the Bible Verse onto the ruled paper strips. Then we are ready.

Right on time, the children begin to arrive.

"Welcome back. Today, we are going to learn another Jesus story."

"Will we have snack?" one of the children asked.

"Yes, we will have a snack at the end. Today, we are going actually to watch what really happened on the screen. It will be like being there."

The screen brighten to show Jesus at 12 years old traveling with Mary and Joseph to Jerusalem for the Passover feast. It's something they did every year. This year, Mary and Joseph started home but Jesus stayed behind. Neither one knew it! Mary thought Jesus was with Joseph and Joseph thought Jesus was with Mary. After a day, they realized it wasn't with them. They looked among all those travelling with them. He wasn't there.

Mary and Joseph returned to Jerusalem and searched. After 3 days, they found him in the Temple. Jesus had been with the teachers. Jesus had been listening and asking questions. The people around had been amazed by him. Mary told him that they had been worried about him. Jesus responded He was to be in his Father's House. They did make it home!

The video ends.

[Luke 2:41-52]

Then the questions started. These children are not unlike I was. They have a great many, many "Why" questions.

"Why didn't they look first in the Temple?"

"Why would they be worried ? Did they not know about His Angels?"

"You know those are great questions and the best time people to ask would be them.   Let's start a list of questions for people and then we will see if they will visit us."

I hang some big flip-chart paper on the wall and write "Mary and Joseph" at the top.

"Okay, let's write our questions down. First one..."

They give me their questions - even Jonathan adds one.

"Is that all for now? We can always add more. Let's do our memory verse."

Jonathan holds up the memory verse and reads it from the strips.

And Jesus grew in wisdom and stature, and in favor with God and men. Luke 2:52

Jonathan asks the children to repeat it with him.

He says "Let's do it Louder." The children comply.

"Is it time for God to hear?" One asks.

"Sure" I say.

As loud as they can, they shout it!

God, Himself, says "All heaven heard it! Good Job!"

The Bible Verse Helper places it on the bulletin board under the first Bible verse we learned. We don't have to repeat the ones from last week. We know them.

"Now that everyone in heaven knows what we are studying, let's move to the table."

Before class, Jonathan and I placed a boy Jesus action figure in each place. It looked just like the video or in this case, the real Jesus little boy.

"From the video, you saw that Jesus wore clothes different from what He wears here or that you might have worn. Jonathan is going to tell us about outfit."

No issues with Jesus undergarments as Jesus was dressed as appropriately this time! The first time I taught this story - we had an issue with what type of undergarment Jesus would have worn. It's too long for this time but catch me after class for more explanation.

I hear laughing in my head (both Buddy and Bubba at the same time!)

The children have finished the action figures and ran to put them in their cubbies.

The Snack Helpers retrieve the cups and napkins.

Jonathan pours the grape juice this time.

I bring out gummies in the shape of little Torahs! After all, it said Buddy put His Words in our mouths; They would not depart. [Isaiah 59:21] Buddy is the creativity one so I knew he would appreciate this one! DEVOUR VERSE!

The children finish and start to depart with their action figures.

Jonathan and I prepare for the classroom for the next session.

Jonathan "I'm starting to wonder what the next snack will be!"

"It's always a mystery!"

LAST CHAPTER: THE HINTS

I slept well after the class day with Susan and our Warehouse tour.

As I woke up, I decided to keep on my comfy pj's for devotions. You can probably guess by now that I had headed for my porch and the Gwennie-size swing.

This time was very different!

Papa and Bubba were waiting in the swing. I should have dressed! I think devotion time is going to be very different this time.

I just make myself at home in the middle like the Gwennie sandwich and lay my head on Papa's shoulder.   We watched the sunrise together without saying a word.

"Gwennie, remember no tears in Heaven."

Papa says "We thought it was time to show you something special. It will be on the video."

"Do you mean everyone will see it?"

Papa : "No, this one is just for you."

"Okay, but could we watch a little of the game first."

"We knew that you would say that. Que the film."

The Score is still 1- 0 in favor of the White Team.

The Black team is at bat. There is a runner on first. The count is 3 balls and 2 strikes. The next pitch is a fastball. It's a swing and a miss! Woo Hoo! One more down.

The next batter comes to the plate. He hits a foul ball. Strike one. The next one hits the foul pole. Strike two. The next one is a little pop-up that the 1st Baseman quickly handles.

The next batter is on deck. He is taking a couple of practice swings trying to stare down the Whites' pitcher. He finally walks into the batter box. The first pitch is a fast ball (the pitcher doesn't seem to change up his game or the catcher doesn't call another kind). The batter connects. I hold my breath. It looks like it's headed for the centerfield wall. The runners are heading around the bases. It could mean the Blacks could score! The Centerfielder races toward the ball. He jumps up with his mitt in the air and connects. He comes down with his arm stretched high! Another OUT!

"Papa, I'm ready for my surprise."

"Let's start the video."

"Gwennie, do you recognize this time?"

"I do. I'm placing a little hint, and no one saw it."

"Do you want to see what happens next?"

"Oh yes, I can't wait to see if anyone caught on."

"You will be surprised."

DISCLAIMER

This book is a dream – how I envision my heaven to be (or maybe Jesus' 1000-year reign on earth, I don't know). It's not meant to add or detract from the real Revelation penned by John. I didn't visit heaven nor have angels appeared to me.

Please read it for yourself. It's amazing so I can only imagine how it will be for us.

I hope to see you there!

glw

DISCUSSION QUESTIONS

POST Book

Second Lunch Discussion Questions:

1. In Luke 1: 32, The Angel tells Mary that Jesus will be great and the Son of the Most High but when he start talking about his Father's House she and Joseph were confused. Why was it confusing that he would say his father's house? I mean it's mentioned in Luke 2:49-50. I wonder what they really thought his "Father's Business" was. Thoughts?

2. Luke Chapter 1 records Mary's song, in which she sings "all generations will call me blessed". Have you ever thought about what that means?

3. Did Joseph ever cuss when he hit his thumb with a hammer in front of Jesus and repent to Him? Do you think that his earthly parents understood the magnitude of his presence?

4. What happened to Joseph? He is mentioned in the birth story and the trip to the Temple. Then when Jesus is rejected at Nazareth [Luke 4: 14-28], Jesus is called the "Son of Joseph". We don't know what happened to him. He isn't mentioned at the cross like Mary.

5. Mary was part of the upper room when Buddy arrived. [Acts 1:14] What did she have to do with the formation of the Church? What was her role after the arrival of the Holy Spirit?

Fourth Lunch Questions:

1. As anyone ever taken a dislike to you because of your faith? What did you do about it?

2. Have you have had a "For Such a Time as This" ? Have you ever had to stand as the light ? Maybe something wasn't right at work and you were the single voice for truth or justice.

3. How as God prepared you for your "For Such a Time as This"?

4. Some think that "For Such a Time as This" is now for the United States. What do you believe ? What can we do as Believers?

Fifth Lunch Discussion Questions:

1. Have you ever had what you felt was an encounter with God? What lead you there? Where were you? Did you receive a specific message?

2. One of the benefits from my encounter was a freedom from a lie. It was all based on a "lie" that I believed from the evil one. What lies have you believed? Has God ever used someone or something to free you from a lie?

www.ingramcontent.com/pod-product-compliance
Lightning Source LLC
Chambersburg PA
CBHW060230180626
46813CB00007B/3036